Pandanus Online Publi
web site, presents additional material relating to this book.

www.pandanusbooks.com.au

THE STONE SHIP

THE STONE SHIP

Peter Raftos

PANDANUS BOOKS
Research School of Pacific and Asian Studies
THE AUSTRALIAN NATIONAL UNIVERSITY

Cover: *De toren van Babel*, Pieter Bruegel de Oude, 1563–1568.
Image courtesy of Museum Boijmans Van Beuningen, Rotterdam, The Netherlands

Typeset in Garamond 10.75pt on 13pt and printed by Pirion, Canberra

National Library of Australia Cataloguing-in-Publication entry

Raftos, Peter.

       The stone ship.

       ISBN 1 74076 135 9.

       I. Title.

A823.4

Editorial inquiries please contact Pandanus Books on 02 6125 3269

www.pandanusbooks.com.au

Published by Pandanus Books, Research School of Pacific and Asian Studies, The Australian National University, Canberra ACT 0200, Australia

A Sullivan's Creek Publication

Pandanus Books are distributed by UNIREPS, University of New South Wales, Sydney NSW 2052 Telephone 02 9664 0999 Fax 02 9664 5420

Editor: Maxine McArthur

Production: Ian Templeman, Justine Molony, Emily Brissenden

for Karen

Acknowledgements

I would like to thank Ian Templeman, without whose encouragement this novel would never have been started, let alone finished. Then there are the wonderful production people at Pandanus, Justine Molony, Duncan Beard, Emily Brissenden, Alex Leonard, Thelma Sims and Jo Bushy. Thank you all for your hard work, patience, kindness and conversation. Maxine McArthur, to whom I owe a debt of gratitude: I could not have hoped for a better copy editor. Also Phillip Winn, thanks for the enthusiastic response to an early draft. Finally, thanks to my wife, Karen Westmacott, who has encouraged me, supported me and inspired me, in this as in everything.

THE ISLE OF GOATS

I had come here to die.

I had not given the method of my death much thought, presuming that I would hang myself or use one of the pistols. As long as I didn't have to cut myself, I could probably go ahead with it.

There was no reason not to go right on and do it now, watched over by the two goats who had taken such an interest in my movements since my arrival on the island. And yet, and yet, I was not quite ready. Perhaps I was too great a coward to face it, so I cast about for reasons to put the act off until later, or the next day.

Frustrated at myself, but not yet ready to die, I started down to the beach and began ferrying my belongings to the hut at the top of the cliff. On the third and final trip, near sunset, I filled my bucket from the spring that trickled out of the cliff face.

I was avoiding death, but it was easier to concentrate on small activities and let the great questions slide for a time. Perhaps I was merely exhausted by my grief. Perhaps I needed to rest before I could place the loaded flintlock just in front of my ear and squeeze the trigger. It had not occurred to me that it was possible to be too tired to die. It was so much easier to collect firewood, to light a fire, boil water, make a hot drink and then a meal as the sun went down. I listened to crickets and furtive night creatures, mostly rodents, as they moved around out in the darkness, and I drank a cupful of plum brandy, watching the sparks rise from my fire.

It was like so many nights, in that I thought I was so tired that I must sleep immediately, and be away from my self for a few hours. But sleep would never come, only thoughts of Alexa, of how much I missed her, of the hunger I felt at the thought of her face, her smell, her touch, her voice. Exhausted from crying and self-loathing, I dozed off, next to the fire.

In the morning I was still trapped with me. Of all the people in the world, the one I least wanted around was me. It is that feeling, I thought, that will make me end it.

On top of everything else, I was stiff from sleeping curled up on the ground by the fire.

Perhaps today was the day, my last day on earth, here on the Isle of Goats. I looked at the trees, the goats, my feet. Everything appeared strangely bright, as though suffused with their own inner light, a light I'd never before noticed: they were precious because soon to be lost. Would this be the last time that I saw these things? Was that the last dawn I would ever see? Would I do it today? Yes, I thought, today is the day. Time to stop putting it off, time to take the rope and loop it around a branch. I squared my shoulders, took a deep breath, and immediately began thinking of excuses to wait until tomorrow.

I decided to use the rope. It took me most of the day to reach that decision, during which time I had wandered over the whole island. It was mostly boulders, crags and tufty, hard-wearing grass. There were a few cypress trees scattered here and there, apart from the grove near my hut. By my estimate there were perhaps twenty or thirty goats living there, most quite shy of me. The two who had greeted me on arrival and slept near the fire accompanied me on my exploration, staying well out of reach but never straying too far.

My feelings about the rope were not altogether rational. I had flintlocks with me, and the ball from one would have been enough to end my self-misery. And the rope was a slow way to go, given that I intended to lower myself gently from a branch, rather than leap and thus break my neck. I'm scared of falling. So I tortured myself for most of the afternoon with imagining how the rope must burn against the throat, how I would struggle for air that wouldn't come through the windpipe, kicking and grasping at the rope with weakening fingers as my tongue swelled and my eyes widened. I imagined losing bowel and bladder control, and the rising panic as darkness — I imagined it must be darkness — smothered my still-open eyes.

In the end, it was the thought of losing bowel control that persuaded me, as night fell, not to hang myself. I hated the thought of my bodily wastes dribbling down my leg and cooling there, particularly if I wasn't already dead. The more I thought about the actual dying part, rather than the romantic image of myself hanging from a branch with a beautiful sunset behind, the less appealing I found it. I dislike pain, and I didn't wish to mix it with dying if I could avoid it.

So, sitting by my campfire for the second night, when I should already be dead, resolved never to see another dawn,

I fished around in my rucksack until I found the pistol case. Inside were the heavy bore flintlocks, military models, inaccurate but deadly: no duellist's weapons, these.

I chose one and dropped a cartridge down the muzzle. The pieces could fire both loose powder-and-shot, and prepared paper cartridges. I had eight cartridges made by the gunsmith. I preferred them to loose ball because they contained a standard charge of powder, strong enough to do the job, but not so strong as to damage the pistol: although I'd had shooting lessons, I didn't completely trust myself to measure out powder from the flask in sufficient quantity to surely kill me without causing the barrel to explode.

I took a swig of plum brandy. Would this be the last time I tasted brandy? The pistol was loaded and cocked, a dull, deadly weight in my lap. I looked at the fire, the stars. In the darkness, I heard a marmot skitter across a rock. The two companionable goats slept under one of the cypresses, just at the edge of the light cast by the fire. One twitched in its sleep, dreaming. There was a clump of grass by my boot, a beetle making its way stolidly between the blades. My back ached and the brandy burnt in my stomach. I knew that I had only a few more minutes to live. I felt that I should think of Alexa, of the life we had not had together, but I couldn't: my mind was completely still, soaking up the living and unliving things around me.

Slowly, I took the pistol in my hand, looking at it in the firelight. This would be the last fire I would ever see, unless they had such things in the underworld.

I looked away, and then raised it to my head. I touched the muzzle to my temple, so that I would not accidentally angle the shot. It was possible, or so I'd heard, to strike the skull glancingly with the ball, which then bounced away, leaving the would-be suicider with a cracked skull and concussion, but alive, perhaps with brain damage. I did not want to make that mistake.

So there I sat, looking at the goats, with the fire on one side and a gun at my temple. Gently, I squeezed the trigger until my finger met resistance as the mechanism engaged, and then I stopped. I was as close to death as I could be. All I had to do was work the muscles of my index finger, and the misery would end. If there truly was an afterlife, then I might even be with Alexa again.

Just a simple act, no more than a slight tug, and then darkness. But what if there wasn't darkness, not immediately? What if the eyes continued to see after death, even if only for a moment? Would the hindquarters of two sleeping goats under a cypress be the first thing I saw in the land of the dead?

Worse yet, what if there was no afterlife, no underworld? What if the ball shattered my brain and everything went black? I tried to imagine a time without me, a future in which I was not, and panic rose as I stared into the abyss of my own non-existence. I had to look away.

I knew then that I could not kill myself, that I did not want to die, even if I did not want to live. I lowered the pistol, thinking with horror of how close I had just come to snuffing out my own light, of making myself cease. I uncocked the mechanism and gingerly, as though it were a sleeping fanged thing, placed it by my side, away from the fire.

I looked up, and saw the man standing just within the circle of firelight. He had been watching me.

'Nice night for it,' he said. 'Or then again, perhaps you've decided it's not?'

I grabbed the pistol and pointed it at him.

'Um,' he said, glancing at the weapon and then back at me. 'You should cock that, if you intend to use it.'

I looked at the pistol. True, it would not fire. And why should I defend myself, if he meant me harm? I had just been within a heartbeat of self-harm, anyway. But I'd decided that I didn't want to die, that I should defend myself. My thoughts made very little sense, but still they chased each other, manically.

'If you're a brigand,' I said, rising to my feet while keeping the still-uncocked pistol pointed vaguely at him, 'then you're welcome to my things, but apart from a little brandy, I don't have much.'

The stranger waved, as though shooing away a fly. 'What would a brigand be doing here, at the arse end of the archipelago? Stealing goats?'

He had a point.

'And,' he went on, 'for someone who might at this moment be dead, but for their own finger, you're a little defensive. May I?' He indicated that he wanted to come closer, into the light. I held my free hand palm upwards to indicate assent, but then aimed the pistol at his heart. If he was not a brigand then he had to be a lunatic because that was the only explanation I could think of for his being here after dark. If I wasn't going to harm myself, I was damned if I was going to let anyone else do it.

He wore the tricorn hat, knee breeches and embroidered waistcoat of the wellborn, although the cut looked to be from my grandfather's time. He did not appear to be armed. I could see a queue poking out from the hat, tied in a black ribbon.

'Who are you?' I asked.

'I might ask the same of you, but my name is Josef Finch.' He removed his hat and bowed in the formal manner.

It was in the reign of the tyrant Ossimene, after the fall of the government of the Plutocrats' Party, that I came to the island. I was not exiled, nor was I under investigation by the secret police, nor was there — to my mind, at least — any question that I was in any way considered a danger or unreliable by the new regime.

No, I came to the island for entirely other, personal reasons: my wife had died in childbirth. Alexa and I were a love-match, an old-fashioned rarity in these enlightened days of arranged marriages. I had met her sister, Miranda, at the training-school for bureaucrats and conceived an infatuation for the dark-eyed beauty. We flirted and exchanged notes, and eventually she invited me to her family home for tea with her mother and sisters. And that was where I met Alexa.

She was no great beauty, my wife-to-be. A flat, round face like a moon, with washed-out grey eyes and hair the colour, but not the consistency, of wet straw. She had a sharp tongue, too, which made my own nervousness and desire to please the mama of Miranda even more painful.

So there we sat, in the sun room, I in my tight suit, as befitted a soon-to-be-graduated government employee, with Miranda to my right and giggling youngest sister Louisa to my left. In front of me, across the table, were the watchful Alexa and Jane, their mother. They were all so graceful and light with the tea things; dainty manners and dainty ways. I had not realised that Miranda came from such a well-bred family; several rungs above my own.

I was the child of hereditary wool merchants. It's true that many wool dealers become inordinately wealthy, but these are the lucky or well-connected or well-born few at the top of the great pile of smaller-scale dealers, those who bark around the edges or act on commission from the great houses. My parents were such barkers and scratchers and so, although we were certainly not poor, nor were we among the rich.

Although I was not one of the rougher sort, in the presence of Miranda, her mother and sisters and especially the caustic Alexa, I felt that there was a clear gap in our social situations, with me on the lower end. Alexa made it clear to me that she agreed. She spoke sharply, and watched me closely, like a hunting bird. Somehow, without a word being spoken or a move being made, she had placed herself in charge of the afternoon tea, a position which should have been occupied by her mama. I was already nervous, and stupidly played along, paying Alexa court rather than her mother or even Miranda, the supposed object of my desires.

She was cruel and sharp and I was a callow youth uncomfortably aware of his own imagined or real inadequacies in a room full of his social superiors. And she almost succeeded in driving me from the house forever. I had been trying to make chitchat, trying not to drop my cup and saucer — aware of the slight rattle of crockery whenever I moved my hand — trying not to drop crumbs or cream on my lap, when Alexa did the thing that, although I did not know it at the time, would eventually lead to us being married.

I had been trying to answer a question from Alexa's mother without spraying the room in cake, while simultaneously juggling my cup and saucer, when there was a crash from across the table. I looked up, and saw Alexa with three-quarters of an eclair and the contents of a cup of tea with lemon splashed across her lap and blouse. I had been dimly aware that everyone was watching my manoeuvre with my cups and plates and food closely, but I had not realised how closely. It seemed that Alexa had gone so far as to forget her own obligations to gravity. I would never have imagined that sharp, clear Alexa could ever do such a thing: I was the clumsy one. She looked down at her ruined dress, then straight at me. Then came the moment that defined Alexa for me, forever. She smiled at me, only at me, and winked.

So I dropped my cup and plate on my lap, too.

I don't know why I did that. Just an impulse, but it was the right impulse.

Years later, when we were lying in bed together, after our third or fourth coupling ever, Alexa told me that she started to fall in love with me from that moment I had dropped my cup and saucer. And I, too, had spent less and less time thinking of her sister and more and more time thinking of Alexa after the incident of the cups.

She admitted to me afterwards that she had deliberately tried to unsettle me because I had looked so serious, because I had been so obviously terrified of doing or saying anything that might have offended the family. It goaded her.

We fell in love, and we stayed in love through the next three years, until she was old enough to marry me and I was secure in my position in the government bureaucracy, with good prospects for advancement. I had passed all the exams, some with distinction. We married and for two years were happy together, although no child appeared. We both longed for a child to present to our parents and to the ancestors, but none came.

Of course, two years was not considered long to wait for conception, especially given the fertility problems that people had in those days. Still, better to have problems at the beginning than at the end of pregnancy, as the saying goes. And we had problems at the end. I still do not know what happened to Alexa or to the baby in the theatre: by ancient law, men are not admitted, so I had to

wait for hours in the cold antechamber. I knew something very bad
had happened when I saw the faces of the the doctor and the
midwives. Oh, they were very consolatory, tried to tell me how
brave Alexa had been and how sorry they were, a million-to-one
chance, something broken inside of her and — they didn't tell me
this, but I could imagine it — blood, blood, so much of Alexa's
blood gushing from her that nothing could keep her in this world.
I never even found out the sex of the baby, stillborn.

I buried my child and my wife on the same day, a sunny
day.

After that, my city became hateful. This city where I had
been born and raised, where my father and mother and
grandfathers and grandmothers and all my other ancestors had
lived, this city where I had been building a career, where my friends
and kin all dwelt: this city now seemed empty, dry like dust. To
leave the city of one's birth voluntarily is a kind of betrayal, but
I could no longer stay. In leaving, I spoke and acted to my family
and in-laws in such a way that I could not now return.

And so I came to the Isle of Goats. There is a chain of
islands, south of the bay which encloses the city, stretching to the
west. The easternmost of these islands are bare and inhospitable,
and are places of enforced exile. But the western islands are more
pleasant: people, citizens of my city, live there by choice, planting
cypresses and olives and growing guavas in hothouses, keeping
goats and rock ponies and donkeys. Out beyond the sweeping arm
of the archipelago is the Isle of Goats. It is small and uninhabited,
except by — as the name suggests — semi-wild goats. In addition,
there are marmot-like rodents. There is a single clear water spring.
Occasionally sealers and fishermen overnight there, because the
reefs to the south and west are excellent hunting grounds, but it's

whispered that the sharks are cunning at extracting men from boats, so expeditions to these reefs are rare.

I came to the island to be alone, to see no more that city which I now both loved and hated. I wanted to be alone with my memories of Alexa. I was not altogether accurate in claiming that I had not been exiled to the island: I had, but not by the tyrant Ossimene. It was self-exile. I came to the island to be alone, to watch the sun rise and the sun set. To be bored, to sit under the cypresses and hate the world, or myself, which amounted to the same thing. And then to kill myself.

———————

'What are you doing on this island?' I asked this fellow, Finch.

He half-smiled at that, a rueful look. 'The same as you.'

Silence. If telling the truth, he too had come to the island to suicide. And he had watched me fail.

Finch took a deep breath, and looked into the fire, both longingly and morosely. 'But unlike you, I succeeded.'

Now, of course I believed in the spirits of the dead, but I had never seen one — surely if I were to, it would be Alexa, and not the ghost of a complete stranger? It was senseless. He was a madman. I decided to humour him.

'You're dead?'

Finch waved his hand into the darkness, where a goat bleated. He might have been waving aside my question or pointing to the trees.

'I hanged myself back there, oh, some years ago. Probably before you were born. Nasty. Don't do it that way,' he paused, glancing meaningfully at my undischarged pistol, 'if you're resolved.'

'You're dead?'

He looked up at me, sharply. He must have realised I did not believe him, because, smiling, he leaned towards the fire. Holding out his right hand, he placed it, open and palm down, into the centre. I watched him hold it down on a burning log. There was no sizzle, no smell of burning meat. He didn't even wince. Then he stepped back and held his arm straight, hand up and palm towards me. It was undamaged.

'You're dead.' I swallowed. No madman, but a real spirit. So there was an afterlife! 'Didn't that hurt?'

He shrugged. 'At the very heart of the fire, I felt a slight warmth, but nothing more. It's dull: I remember that colours were brighter, leaves green, eyes blue or brown. Now they're all washed out, mostly faded sepia. And I can't smell anything.'

'But,' I said, motioning for him to sit down, 'there's life after death? There's an underworld?'

We sat. I put away my pistol.

He looked rather sad, or perhaps bored. 'Look, I don't want to be difficult about this, but that's an almost impossible question to answer. Is there an afterlife? Possibly. I don't know. If that's what I'm having, it's not much and I don't recommend it. If you want my advice, stay alive as long as you possibly can because the alternative, as far as I've seen, is pretty lousy.'

His answer made no sense.

'But you're from the underworld.'

Finch raised an eyebrow. 'Friend, I haven't been able to get off this island since I died.'

Well, so much for the spirits of the dead being able to travel anywhere and return in a single night.

'So you can bring me no news of Alexa?'

He screwed up his face and hugged himself. He shook his head and said, 'Who?'

This shade brought no news of the underworld, no news of Alexa. Presumably he did not know my ancestors, either. He seemed a very second rate kind of ghost, of no use to me. I suppose I should have been more impressed with being in the presence of the undead, but for all I could see, he was just getting in the way of my moping. After all, I had come here to be alone. 'Why are you here?' I asked.

At that, Finch looked up with interest. 'Ah. My young friend, you came very close to death at your own hand a little while ago.' He gazed back at the fire. 'And so the line between the living and the dead became momentarily thinner. I'm close to the living, you see. And you came close to the dead.'

He looked up and gazed at me with a dopey look, as though the explanation were complete.

I waited. Another goat bleated.

'And … ?' I asked.

'Hmm?' He blinked, and looked around as though just remembering where he was. He dusted imaginary dust off his breeches. 'Oh, yes. The 'and'. There's always an 'and', I'm afraid.'

We gazed at each other.

He looked embarrassed. 'Oh, the "and". What's your name?'

I told him: 'Shipton'.

'Well, Shipton, the point is this. I killed myself, but I'm still angry about the circumstances that preceded my death, the circumstances that convinced me that the only path open was suicide. You follow?'

I nodded.

'Good. Since killing myself did not in any way end my suffering, I've decided that I want revenge. I want him dead, the bastard who is responsible for my being a disembodied spirit stuck on an island of goats and marmots. Marmots are dull, do you know that?

'I've been waiting ever so long. And now you came along.'

I saw no reason to become involved in a ghost's vendetta, and objected. He cut me off with a raised finger.

'You don't want to live, do you?' he asked.

I didn't answer. I didn't know the answer.

'Let me put that another way: you are so tired of yourself and your grief that you can't imagine how you can go on being you in your own head.'

I looked down. We both knew the answer.

'Mmm. Know the feeling. You can't go on, but you can't die, either.'

Again, we both knew the answer.

'Well, I took several days before I could throw rope over branch. Unpleasant way to go, I'd use a pistol next time. As though there were going to be a next time.'

I looked up, sharply. I doubt he was being sarcastic: he was turned inward, thinking of his own death.

He came out of himself. 'This Alexa you mentioned, I suppose she's dead.'

I nodded.

'I'm sorry for that.' he said, and sounded sincere. 'You're not yet thirty years old, are you?'

I looked back at the fire and nodded again.

Finch rubbed his hands, trying to warm them by the flames. 'And yet, and yet, it seems to you now that life is over. Without your Alexa, how can you continue?'

I looked up again. How could I go on without her?

Finch straightened, his hands towards me, palms upraised as though in supplication. 'The days stretch out, a grey and empty road. All the days alone, the nights alone. I know, I know that. How must it feel for you? Days of misery, sadness and rage struggling inside you, no room for anyone or anything else.'

I swallowed, fighting back the tears. How did he know what it was like for me?

'At last the night comes, and you hope for sleep to take away the pain. But the nights are worse, hours of sleepless, empty aching. By day you long for night to hide in, and at night you wish for day so that you can lose yourself in work, crowds.'

He paused, watching me. Then: 'Are there blowflies that go around and around in your head?'

I swallowed again and it was like swallowing a stone.

'Yes,' I sighed or sobbed.

Finch waved one hand. 'They won't go away. I had to hang myself to make them shut up.'

Was there no way out?

'You won't forget. It just goes on and on and on. I am here to tell you that relief comes only with exhaustion, and then it all returns. You want it to go away, yes?'

'Yes,' I said, fighting past the catch in my throat, the sobs, the self-pity.

'And,' he said, looking at me in a way I had never seen from anyone, not my family or hers, 'Really, what you want is for it to have never happened, for this to be rubbed out, to have Alexa back.'

I covered my face in my hands, ashamed at my tears. It was all true.

Finch spoke again, and his voice was silk. 'Cry, it's good to cry. Ah, yes. For the rest of your life you will feel it. And when you think you can suffer no more than you already do, you'll see something that reminds you of her when you least expect it. A stranger with similar hair. Shipton, I know.'

I rocked back and forth, hugging myself. I didn't care whether Finch spoke the truth, what he said was beautiful.

'So. Can't live, can't die. Can't go on, can't go back. Would you like my advice?'

I waited. I had cried myself out.

'Well,' he said, drawing a breath, a strange act for the dead. 'Take revenge.'

I looked at the fire, at Finch. I needed him, needed his words. 'But there's nobody to take revenge on.'

'Oh yes there is.' He held up a finger and, across the firelight, his eyes became very large and very bright, like a cat's. Light surrounded him and any lingering doubts I may have had about him being a shade evaporated. 'Yes there is.'

He spoke slowly, feeling the full weight of each word. 'There is the whole world. All of them. The living. If they did not exist, you would not have to feel the misery, the futility.'

Finch lied, but at the same time there was something in what he said.

'And at the same time you can do me a service. You can start with the man who put me here.'

Yes, he spoke the truth in his lies. To have revenge on all the world, on Finch's killer and eventually on myself. And that way I would ultimately have revenge on Alexa, who I wanted to hurt for daring to die, to leave me.

'Oh yes,' said Finch. 'On Alexa too.'

'And the pain will go away?' I asked.

Finch paused. 'I will not lie to you. I cannot promise that revenge will take away the pain. But it will provide its own pleasures.'

I smiled. So did Finch. He said he would not lie, but we both knew that he had lied. His lies were persuasive, but that is not the same as truth. How could I do other than what I did? I had run out of possibilities: I knew that I would not kill myself, and yet having left my city and my family, I could not return to them, could not face the shame. Finch offered me a path, and I did not think too hard about where that might lead. If he lied, then his lies were better than truth. If I was weak, then better to serve someone strong. And, besides, I had nowhere else to go. I smiled, and my smile was an oath to serve him. He smiled, and his smile was an oath to repay my service.

And that is how I came to be in Finch's service, a revenger for a ghost.

A JOURNEY
OF REVENGE

It is said that, before setting out on a journey of revenge, one should first dig two graves. My feelings about travelling to a distant land in order to kill a complete stranger on behalf of a ghost were somewhat mixed. I sometimes agreed with Finch's reasoning that if one could neither go forward nor backward then the only option was to seek rage and revenge; and then at times that sounded like so much nonsense. It was hard for me to decide, since I didn't know when I was in my right mind: the different arguments held sway depending on my mood. And my moods were uniformly bleak, but variable in their degrees of anger and exhaustion.

Also, I wasn't sure whether I was even capable of killing another human being, much less one I didn't know. Oh, there were times when I felty angry enough to do it, but I was no killer: I was a career bureaucrat who had lost his wife. When it came to the crunch, could I really kill someone, anyone? So far, I had proved unable to harm myself, but that wasn't the same thing: just as we all secretly love the smell of our own farts, but gag at the smell of others', so we all hold our own lives in infinite esteem, far more so than even the lives of those we love. If nothing else, I knew that I would not really change places with Alexa. If one of us had to die, then better by far that it be she.

My doubts about Finch's revenge were greatest during the day, when the sun was warm and shadows held no secrets but were merely themselves. It was at night, when Finch came to me, sometimes in dreams, sometimes in his own shape as he had at the Isle of Goats, that the whole trip seemed obvious, and simple, and necessary. His need for revenge seemed so persuasive in those times. He would chuckle and, with a word or two, ease away my doubts.

By now I had left the island and was en route to the town of Moritz, several weeks' journey north of my city. It was here, according to Finch, that we were to seek his revenge. And Finch had come with me. I can't say whether the ghost of Finch travelled with me, or whether he had somehow bedazzled me and remained trapped on the Isle of Goats: he was quick to deflect such questions.

We travelled with a caravan because the wooded lands between cities is often unsafe. The caravan master was a dumpy one-eyed man by the name of Horne who affected cavalrymen's whiskers and carried a sabre. He was well-respected by the other travellers, a veteran of wars and dangerous caravan routes. I suspect my fellow-travellers thought me mad, since at night I made my own fires away from them and talked to myself. It was clear that the others could neither see nor hear Finch. If anything, I was valued, because madmen are supposed to bring luck to caravans.

Apart from Finch — who may not count as a person — and myself, the 'we' included a mule I had acquired. This creature spent its evenings stolidly munching on oats or grass, considering me with a sadness that suggested that she, too, thought I was mad, and in her estimation, a madman was an impossibly sad thing. During the day she carried my belongings, but absolutely refused to carry me, although she been eager enough to carry her previous owner when I bought her.

So there I was, footsore and taken for a harmless madman, with a ghost and disapproving mule for companions.

'Why are you seeking revenge, Finch?' I asked, as I scraped my boots.

He sat opposite me, across the fire. As always, he hugged himself close and leaned forward, trying to warm himself — hopeless task — at the flames.

'Bah. It's obvious, isn't it?'

Even as his reasons became more flimsy to my ear, they carried greater weight with my stomach. My head cried out that it was not obvious and my heart stirred, smelling the promised blood.

'Yes. Obvious.'

He looked up sharply, trying to gauge whether my answer was sarcastic. It was not, but there was no way that Finch could tell this.

'There is a man, who was once my friend, who took from me everything. Everything, you understand?' That earnest look. 'Honour, love, happiness, money, reputation. He destroyed me as completely as you might throw an ant into that fire. All he left me was my life.'

There was a pause. The mule's ears twitched as she dozed, and somewhere behind me men and women laughed softly. Someone was telling a story back there.

Finch continued. 'He left me my life. He didn't take it, so I did.'

He was exaggerating: whenever Finch spoke of his reasons for suicide, he always framed them in sweeping generalities —

honour, his good name, love — words he spoke in such a way that I could hear the capital letters. Finch never used specifics, never named names. Huge unspecified wrongs had been perpetrated on him, and he'd responded by making for himself a hemp collar. Finch inhabited extremes.

'Finch, how can you possibly have revenge? How could you inflict anything that equals to your suffering?'

'Oh,' he said, in answer to my question, half smiling, 'There are ways.'

'And why won't you tell me who we are seeking? And do you really intend for me to kill him?'

In reply, Finch merely spread his hands and smiled again: discussion closed.

I gave up for the night and lying down, rolled myself into my blanket. I fell asleep to the soft snores of the mule. In the morning, as ever, Finch was gone, but I knew he'd be back the following night.

And so it went, night after night, interrupted only by those infrequent stops at small towns along our route, where the merchants would set up shop, buying and selling, while we other travellers explored. I had never seen other towns, and although they were smaller and much shabbier than my old city, the sights and smells made me homesick for my homeland. I thought I had done with that place forever, but I realised, fleetingly, that it was still my home, and perhaps it always would be. Shame could be borne. It was also the only place where I could properly honour Alexa's shade: for the first time, I realised that in all this I was being impious. If Finch was a shade, then surely Alexa was too, and she needed me to burn incense for her. And I could only do that back in my city.

I had smiled at Finch and so sworn an oath to serve him, but as the caravan travelled further away from my home city and from the Isle of Goats, my commitment wavered more and more. After all, Finch was a ghost and so any arrangement with him probably wasn't binding. Besides, we had signed no contract. I resolved to escape.

It was insanely dangerous to travel alone on these roads, what with the brigands. I decided to wait in the next town we came to until I found a caravan heading back. I wouldn't have long to wait: we were on one of the main regional trade routes.

The next town was called 'Pell' or 'Quell'. We arrived just on nightfall. There were three or four travellers' pens just below where the town's walls would have stood, in the old days before artillery made them obsolete. The pens were simple enclosed spaces with their own wells and a thatch roof running along three sides and there was no cost to use them.

We watered and fed our animals, made supper, and then bedded down for the night.

Having decided to make my escape I was restless and, after tossing for a while, crept out into the open space in the middle of the pen. Everything seemed harsh and flat under the moonlight. Trying to walk quietly, so as not to wake the others, I turned out of the pen and into the night.

With the town and pens to my right, I wandered along by a stream and then up a slight, wooded rise to a bare hilltop. From here, I could see across the town to the open country beyond. Leaning against a tree trunk, I thought about that open space: in that direction I would not go, not tomorrow, not ever.

Something moved at the edge of my vision. Turning, I saw Finch, his arms crossed. He was staring at something above me, smiling. The hairs rose on my head.

'Evening, Shipton.' He bowed.

'Oh, Finch,' I replied. 'Where did you come from?'

The spectre waved a hand as though to dismiss the question.

'Did you think that was a tree, friend Shipton?' He pointed at what I was leaning against.

Confused, I stepped away. I saw that I had not been leaning against a tree, but a stout timber pole, reinforced by cross-struts near the ground. With my eyes, I followed it up and then along the attached crossbeam to the end. I shuddered and jumped away.

Finch chuckled at my discomfit. 'I can tell you from personal experience that mandrake definitely does not grow beneath a hanged man.'

I took a few more steps away from the gallows.

The ghost looked me up and down.

'If I might make a personal observation,' he began, 'there are times in one's life when great changes occur. Perhaps travel or,' he raised an eyebrow, 'the death of a loved one.'

I waited. I was not looking forward to this conversation. What might he do to me when I told him I would not be going on?

'I'll get to the point.' He walked past me until he was standing directly under the gallows. 'At such times, we may begin to have second thoughts, and wish — however fleetingly — to turn aside from a course of action on which we have embarked. Or we may believe that a deal is not a deal, that having given our word, we can retract.'

Finch stopped, turned away to the view of the town. 'Are you having second thoughts?'

Here was my opportunity. 'Forgive me, Finch, but I am not going on with this.'

The spectre did not move. After a time, he said, 'Then leave.'

So it was that easy. I had expected some resistance, an argument, perhaps even pleading. Instead of relief, I felt almost disappointed. Did he not want me? Was I that incidental? I walked away from him, down the hill, thinking that I was no use, not even to a ghost.

I could now return home, to my family and Alexa's family. I would be able to sacrifice to Alexa's memory. Perhaps I could regain my old job. But there would be recriminations: I abandoned my family and her family in a time of need and grief. Would I be forgiven? It seemed less and less likely. Perhaps they wouldn't even meet with me. And what of the secret police? They would want to know what I had been up to while outside the city. Had I been in contact with the surviving enemies of the tyrant Ossimene? Once I had fallen into the clutches of the secret police, would I emerge again?

I stopped halfway down the hill, suddenly irresolute. I was a lone traveller with a mule. I knew almost nothing about the world beyond my own city, and would have trouble defending myself against brigands if I travelled alone. It might be a long time before a caravan heading towards my city came by: the caravaneers had said it was a well-travelled route, but why should I believe them? They were strangers, not kin or countrymen. Yet if I stayed with them, I could at least be certain of reaching my destination, whatever that destination was.

I turned and looked back up the path. The moon had gone behind clouds and it seemed suddenly easier to head back up to the clearing than to continue on into the thicker woods below. Anything could be down there.

It wasn't as though I was surrendering to Finch, wasn't as though I considered our bargain binding.

I turned back, up the hill towards him.

I could still get out of it. This simply wasn't the most convenient time.

I came out into the clearing. Finch was exactly as I had left him. I crossed the open ground to the gallows and stood beside him, looking out at the town. I felt strangely content: it was easier not to have to make the decision to leave him immediately. All in good time.

'It's an interesting question,' began Finch. 'To what extent do we have free will, if at all? Or are our lives determined and we have nothing but the illusion of free will?'

'I'm free,' I said, too quickly.

Finch smiled. 'Has it occurred to you, friend Shipton, that we might not be separate? What if we are two halves of the same mind?'

The ghost paused, and his smiled changed to one of malice. 'I suppose it would be an unhinged mind.'

I looked into the cold, hungry eyes of a ghost, trying to gauge his meaning. I knew his idea to be false: 'I remember a time when I had not met you.'

'Memories might be illusions. So might decisions.' The spectre adjusted his hat, and I could no longer see his face. 'You went down the hill, thought of all the difficulties ahead, and changed your mind. Of course you are coming along, going on this journey to help me, out of your own free will.'

Finch told me that it was time for me to get some sleep and so, out of my own choice and not because he'd told me, I returned to the pens and, no longer restless, slept near my mule.

After three weeks, the caravan reached Moritz, which lay in the centre of a fertile plain, mostly fields sown with hemp and barley, with deep forests to the north and west. The plain was watered by an ancient, creaking river. The town was really quite large, perhaps half the size of my own city. Even from kilometres away, I could see that the overarching principle of Moritz was crookedness: the streets were crooked, the roofs were crooked. Even the trees seemed to have strange angles in them.

As we approached the town, Horne turned his horse to the back of the caravan, where I travelled. He pulled up next to me as I walked, leading my mule. The mule snorted.

'Ho, Shipton,' he hailed me.

I looked up, smiled, and nodded.

'Up ahead is the town of Moritz, as you've probably gathered by now. That is where we part company.'

I nodded again, the sun in my eyes. I wondered why he was talking to me now, when he had all but ignored me the entire trip.

'I want you to understand something. You've been a good lunatic, as lunatics go.'

'Thank you,' I said.

'No, no, you misunderstand: that's not what I want to tell you. That's why I'm telling you.'

As I was shading my eyes with my free hand I couldn't see his face very well.

'Be careful,' he continued, 'be careful of your companion. The spirit.'

I was flabbergasted. So Horne could see Finch?

'You can see him?' I asked.

Horne nodded. 'But it's bad luck to talk of these things. You'll be ill-used. Just take care.'

'Wait,' I said, as Horne spurred his horse forward. 'What do you mean?'

Horne, now slightly ahead of me, shook his head and waved a hand backwards, indicating that he did not wish to further discuss it.

I should have asked Horne what he meant, found out whether he could see Finch or sense his presence in some other way. There was a lot that I should have said or asked, but already it was too late to speak or ask: the opportunity, had it ever existed, had already come and gone. The man's back, as he trotted ahead, was all the answer I would get from him. Superstitious or prudent, he would not be drawn.

For now, I had to enter the town and find lodgings. In the morning, I promised myself, I would seek out Horne and find out what he knew or had guessed. And I was going to demand more information from Finch, or else I really would refuse to continue. After all, he needed me.

So we came to Moritz: me, a mule, a ghost and my memories of Alexa. On the journey, I had become convinced that she was beyond me now, no matter that Finch's presence — if it could be called a presence — was evidence of life after death. Perhaps she did survive, in some dim way analogous to Finch's hungry vagueness, or perhaps she was in some far heaven or elysian field. I wondered, though, whether Finch's refusal to cease being was a unique case, and that all other tales of ghosts were fiction. Finch himself, of course, was not forthcoming. Whether he had encountered any other undead, I could only guess.

The town was full of crooked streets, paved with crooked cobbles, and walked by crooked men and women, crooked dogs and cats. Was there a straight line in the place? Everywhere I looked, horizontals crazed, verticals fractured.

Eventually I found a tavern, its walls leaning crazily into the street, its chimneys startled zigzags against the overcast afternoon sky. The room was passable, and I made certain that my mule was fed and watered in the stables outside. I was here in Moritz, as instructed by Finch. Now what? I had to wait until the evening to find that out.

I was staring at the fire in my room, trying to remember what Alexa looked like. Her face and hands, the most expressive parts of her, seemed less distinct. Was I forgetting? It scared me.

I glanced away from the fire, and there was Finch, facing away from me, hands clasped at the small of his back, apparently looking out the window.

There was quiet. It was Finch's prerogative to speak first. The fire popped.

'Moritz,' said Finch, at last. 'How I remember this town.'

There was a pause again, and I turned back to the fire.

'Tell me,' he said. And was that longing in his voice? 'Did Moritz seem a trifle, well, crooked to you?'

I glanced up. He was looking at me over his shoulder. Out of stubbornness and perversity, I said what I said next: I shook my head, turning down the corners of my mouth to indicate dubiety. 'No, not at all. What do you mean?'

He turned back to the window.

'Listen,' he said, and there was something in his voice that I hadn't heard in weeks, not since our first conversation on the Isle of Goats, 'don't ever lie to me. I can tell, do you understand?'

I looked back at the fire.

'I mean it. Moritz is crooked, is it not?'

I turned back to him. He was facing me full, now. His hands were fists at his side.

'I can't say that I've noticed any crookedness. The place is like a plumb line.' I half smiled.

My eyes caught his. What colour were they? Red?

He spoke very slowly. 'Repeat this: Moritz is crooked.'

'You know, Finch, I don't believe it is. I think it's straight.'

Those eyes. Red and redder.

'Yes, Moritz is crooked. Say it.'

'No, Finch. It's straight.' I had been joking, but with neither of us backing down out of good nature, the debate had turned serious.

Redder still. I tried to look away: I couldn't.

'Can you deny the evidence of your own eyes?' And when he said eyes, his own blazed. My throat hurt, itching as though it wanted to say the words he repeated: 'Moritz is crooked.'

'No, Finch,' I said. 'This is childish. We're here now, what do you want?' And still I could not turn away from those eyes.

'Say it.'

'All right!' I yelled. Then I stopped, shrugged, as though it were a matter of little concern. 'It is as you say: Moritz is crooked.'

Finch smiled.

Someone knocked on the door: it was the publican. He had been passing and heard my shout. Was the honoured traveller in need of anything? No, thank you, I replied. I had merely tripped on my own boots and it was my oath that he heard. There was no need for him to be concerned, I was quite all right and had no need of anything. The publican bowed and left. I got up, passing Finch, and latched the door.

When I went back to my chair, Finch moved to the fireplace. He stared into the warmth with that peculiar hunger he seemed to always have whenever he was near flame.

'Well, Finch, what now? We are in your crooked town.'

'Do you know, I was born here,' he said.

Of course I did not know that.

Quietly, he sang a song that he must have learnt as a child in this town. It was a list of streets, and what trade was conducted on each. Then he turned to me again and smiled, a strangely satisfied look on his face. His eyes reflected only the red of the fire, I saw now.

'Every child in Moritz is taught that song. It teaches one their rightful place in the world. On which street do you think I was born?'

I responded that I didn't know. I wasn't sure I cared and, even if I did, I couldn't remember what street carried what trade.

He spread his hands and stared at them. 'I suppose it's not really important. Sleep well, friend Shipton. Tomorrow we leave Moritz.'

So this was not our destination. 'Where are we going?'

'To the University.'

'What university?' There was one in my city.

'The University. It is east of here, perhaps two days. There may be a group of students leaving. If not, engage a guide. The journey is safe, as I remember.'

'Finch, what is the name of this university?' The one at my city had been named after its founder.

He looked at me as though I were mad. 'There is only one University. It has no other name, it has need of no other.'

'Finch, who are we looking for? Are they in the University, or is this just a detour?'

Finch looked at me as though I'd crawled out from under a rock. 'The University is the end. Our revenge is there.'

Later, as I lay in bed, gazing at the coals in the fireplace, I tried to understand the incident about Moritz. Why had Finch been so adamant that I agree with him about Moritz? His description of the town was accurate, and I had only disagreed out of perversity. Yet, instead of letting it pass or treating it as a joke, he had been serious: he was defending a challenge to his authority. So perhaps my eventual deferral to his opinion was more significant than I wanted to acknowledge. One thought scared me: it was possible that I had submitted because I had no choice. At the gallows outside Pell, had I really decided to continue, or had Finch somehow controlled me? Was I losing my free will? I did not want to think about it, but I had enjoyed submitting. I hadn't insisted he tell me who I was to kill, or why. I'd been out-manoeuvred.

The next morning, I paid my bill, put my bags over the mule, and we went to the market. As Finch suggested, I was looking for a caravan or scholars' group to travel with to the University. I wasn't travelling alone with just a guide if I could help it: I am no fighter, and guides are not necessarily trustworthy.

I didn't give much thought to why I was going on with this, except that, having come all this way, I was curious to see the University. I was not doing it because Finch told me to; of that I was certain.

There was a group of students leaving for the University that morning. It was not hard to find them. They were all sitting on a raised stage in the market, singing and yelling, hard to miss in their brown robes. Some had tonsures, others were shaven-headed, others wore their hair long and loose or in braids. Men and women, they were already drunk, although it was not yet nine o'clock.

Near them, seated on a tall stool that rose out of the crooked cobbles and dung, sat a crooked-looking woman in a pointy hat behind an equally tall and crooked desk. She wore half-spectacles and was chewing on a pencil. I guessed that she was in charge of the group, since somebody sober was needed to get them on their way.

I made my way to the desk. By standing on my toes, I could just get my nose over the edge.

The woman at the desk raised her eyebrows, but said nothing.

'Excuse me,' I began.

'Hmmmm?' she said, chewing on her pencil. Her lips were stained.

'I am looking to get to the University.'

'Ahhhhhhh.' She sighed deeply.

'Who should I talk to?'

She bit down too hard on the pencil. There was a sharp crack and it broke in her mouth.

She shook her head, sadly. Then she shrugged, looked to the sky, looked at me, shrugged again, and let loose the deepest, saddest sigh I have ever heard.

'Should I wait with the students?' I nodded towards the drunken scholars.

'Erk,' said the woman. She waved the pencil in the air and the broken end fell away, bouncing off my nose. 'Hum,' she said.

I looked behind me, hoping there was someone else I could talk to. My mule stood at my feet, gazing up at me with an expression that suggested that this was all my problem and there was nothing the mule could do about it, even if she wanted to.

'Ten o'clock,' said the woman.

I looked back. 'Is that when the students leave?'

The woman nodded. 'Want a job, then?'

I didn't understand her.

'A job. A position, a place, yeah?' She began chewing on her pencil again.

'Thank you,' I replied, 'but I am travelling to the University, not looking for work.'

'Well, what are you going there for, then? Can't get in if you're not a scholar. Or got a job.' She looked at me, significantly.

I had not thought of this. If Finch had been a scholar, he might not have realised that the University would not allow me entry, a stranger with no references or reason to be there. Universities can be very hostile places.

I must have looked crestfallen. The woman sighed again, then made a noise like a child playing with a kitten. 'No, no, no. No job, no studies, no way in.' She giggled.

I waited, looking up at her.

She sighed. 'I can help. Yes I can. The gatekeeper's me cousin,' and she started chewing on her pencil, watching me speculatively.

I could see where this was heading. 'How much then, for your good will?'

She smiled, and named a sum. It was not so bad. I handed up the coins.

'Agh,' she muttered to herself, then scribbled something. 'Give this —' she passed me a handwritten note '— to the man they call Strigge. He's the worker's entrance gatekeeper. Tell him Cousin Imelda sent you.'

I thanked her and tipped my hat.

'Yeah, they're always looking for a few more workers there. Probably start you in the kitchens, I 'spect.'

Since I had an hour before the students were due to set out, I decided to try and find Horne. I wanted to talk to him about Finch, draw him out, if possible, on what he knew. It was likely that the caravan was still in the town, since we had only arrived the day before and they would presumably do business here for a while. I guessed they'd be somewhere in this market, assuming there wasn't another one somewhere around the town.

I picked up the mule's lead and, one hand resting on my concealed purse, set out into the crooked throng. I had a sudden suspicion that Cousin Imelda might have been trying to trick me, and so after I was out of her sight, I unfolded the note. After reading it, it seemed innocuous enough, a greeting to her cousin Strigge, and a wish that he would find a job for the bearer of the note somewhere in the University, something not too menial, for I seemed to her to be a gentleman. Then a mark I took to be her signature. Satisfied, I refolded it and put it in my coat.

It took me a little while, but I eventually found some of the traders with whom I had travelled. They smiled at me and nodded in that indulgent way; after all, I was just a madman. A lucky one, though. After we had exchanged greetings, I asked them if they knew where Horne was. Most shook their heads, but one grizzled old fellow said that a caravan had left before dawn for parts west, beyond the Caperian Desert. He thought Horne may well have left on that caravan, seeing as he was one of the best caravan masters in the region. I thanked him, and cursing myself for a fool for not talking to the caravan master when I had the chance, headed back to the carousing students.

They were still there. A few others, dressed like menials, had by now collected under the raised platform, out of the drizzle. I went there too. Although it was fairly smelly under the platform, it was at least dry. The students were ignoring the rain. I nodded to Cousin Imelda, now under a huge umbrella that covered both her and her raised writing desk, but she either ignored or did not see me.

A young woman in a dark cloak gave the mule a carrot. She patted its nose. 'Nice mule,' she said, appreciatively. The mule nuzzled against her hand, either for more caresses or more carrots.

I nodded to her. 'Thank you.'

'Does she have a name?'

'No. She's just a mule.'

'Well, you should give her a name. Even if it's just "Mule".'

In spite of myself, I smiled. 'Very well, I shall call her "Just Mule".'

She stopped, suddenly serious. 'That's not what I meant.'

'Ah, but that is the result of your initial attempt at a good deed. Unintended consequences, perhaps harm,' said a voice from above us. We looked up and saw an upside-down head peering at us from what I had begun to think of as the students' enclosure. It was a chubby face with fat lips and a smug, if drunk, expression.

The woman looked away. 'Philosophy students!' It was a curse.

She walked to the other side of the undercroft, which faced onto a set of holding pens for pigs. Not knowing anyone else, I followed, with Just Mule in tow.

'Excuse me,' I ventured. Above us somebody was singing a bawdy ditty.

She turned back to me, and smiled.

'I'm sorry for the louts above,' I said. I told her my name and held out my hand.

'Moira,' she said. She reached across to Just Mule and stroked the animal's muzzle.

More people joined in the ditty, above. It told of a clever student, a naïve innkeeper, the innkeeper's impressionable daughter, an unpaid bill, free will and determinism.

Moira looked up and shrugged. She turned back to me.
'Never trust a philosophy scholar, never get into discussion with
them. They learn all the tricks. They're trouble, like the lawyers.'

She stopped patting Just Mule and looked at me, her
eyebrows knitting. 'Why are you going to the University?'

I looked down at my hands, suddenly shy. Why indeed?
'I'm looking for work there.'

'Oh,' she said. 'That's not so easy. Have you a letter of
recommendation?'

I showed her the note that Cousin Imelda had scrawled for
me. She read it, then waved it about her head, clucking.

'Well,' she said, handing the note back to me, 'it's better
than nothing, but not much better. That woman has no influence.
How much did you pay for this?'

I told her, and she shook her head. 'Fair price if you get a
position, but if you don't …' She whistled through her front teeth
for a moment. The ditty reached its climax. Moira glanced
upwards, and then back to me. She looked embarrassed, a slight
flush on her pale cheeks. Then she asked, 'What can you do?'

'Do?'

'Yes. Skills, you know.'

'Ah, well, I worked in a government department for a
number of years. I have good clerical and policy skills,' I felt
somehow inadequate.

'Oh,' she said, fluttering her fingers, 'perhaps you'll find
work after all. This is the University, after all.'

Now I was confused.

'Well,' she smiled, 'Maybe you'll be lucky. Try to stay out of
the Science Faculty, if you can. I've heard some very strange stories
about that place.'

'Where do you work?' I asked, wanting to change the subject.

She smiled even more broadly, and pulled aside her cloak slightly to reveal the hooded grey robe she wore. 'In the Library! I am a Librarian, Second Grade. Working in the Circle of Natural History. I was promoted just before I took my holidays. Mama and Papa were so proud!'

She cocked her head to one side. 'Can you read?'

'Yes,' I replied. After all, I was a trained bureaucrat.

'Well, perhaps I can put in a good word for you at the Library. It's better than working in student administration or the kitchens.' She shuddered, and I decided that I should stay away from the kitchens if I possibly could.

Just then wagon wheels hove into view, and a number of large covered carriages, drawn by shire horses, pulled up next to the platform. A stout man with dark glasses and a handbell climbed down from one of the carriages. He pulled out a sheet of paper from his cloak, unfolded it. He commenced reading names from a list on the sheet and, for each one, someone above us yelled 'aye'. From time to time, the named person was apparently absent, because then several would yell 'nay' all together.

After this, the students climbed down from the platform and tramped into the carriages.

Moira grabbed my arm and led me to the back of one of the carriages. She hailed the driver, and he nodded that I could tie Just Mule behind, then we climbed on the roof. A little while later we set off, heading due east towards an apparent smudge, low in the sky, right on the horizon.

Finch had said that it took nearly two days to reach the University from Moritz, but in fact it took the better part of only a single day. We travelled through gentle hedge country, made up for the most part of barley, hops and marigold fields, separated by small copses that were left for rabbits and other small game to breed in. There was a fair amount of traffic on the road and I saw why Finch had judged it to be safe, even for someone as untravelled as me.

Moira told me that she was entitled to return to the family for a short period once a year, and it was these that she called her 'holidays'. I was surprised at this: I hadn't given the working conditions of University employees much thought, but I suppose I had imagined them to be something akin to servants, as they were at the university in my home city. And certainly, back there, servants were not released for visits to their family except for a mortal sickness.

A fourth child of a farming family from near Moritz, I gathered that Moira's family were reasonably well-to-do, perhaps gentlemen farmers, because they could afford to educate their children. She had shown some aptitude for academic work, so the family had called in its favours and spent the money and Moira, for her part, had worked hard and been accepted into the University general staff, within the Library system.

The Library provided the reading material for the entire University, a huge, sprawling effort that required, from what Moira told me, a fiendishly complex accession system. It took decades to truly master this system, and as Moira had been working there only a few years, she was familiar with only its rudiments. Her knowledge was only sufficient to assist lost undergraduates from the Humanities and Natural History. Still, she said optimistically, the system was difficult, but not designed to injure. With time and practice, she'd master it.

Just as the accession system was vast, so too was the Library. It was arranged, so she said, in a series of concentric circles, including the Circle of Natural History, where she worked. Not everyone was allowed to access every Circle, with most students and librarians limited to publications held in the outermost Circles, those of Natural History, Design, Art and the Humanities (excluding Philosophy and Literary Criticism, which holdings were held in other Circles). Apparently the Circles reflected the intrinsic worth of the various branches of knowledge, or at least the degree to which they were held in importance by the University academic and administrative hierarchies. So the outermost circles were the least important schools of learning, while the inner circles contained holdings for such subjects as Philosophy, Semantics and Economics. It was rumoured, she said, that there were innermost Circles of knowledge that belonged to disciplines without names, and to these semi-mythical holdings, only the chief librarians were entitled to go.

It was not clear to me whether the Circles were administrative concepts or actual, physical rings in a building: at times Moira described them in a way that strongly suggested they were concrete, and at other times it seemed to me, from the way she spoke, that this could not be so. Apparently the relative importance of the outermost disciplines was a contentious matter, and there were constant struggles among the academic staff for precedence. The outcome of such battles could necessitate wholesale reorganisation of accession numbers and shelving allocations. In fact, much of the work of librarians of the first three grades was to carry out such reorganisations under the supervision of more senior librarians. There were apparently twenty-four grades of librarian. Regarding the struggles for academic precedence, it was not clear whether these ever took the form of actual, physical violence.

I was confused by Moira's description of the Circles as reflecting the intrinsic worth of various branches of knowledge.

While I understood that disciplines, as represented by administrative organisations, could be considered of lesser or greater importance, and that internal political wrangling could change the relative importance of administrative units, it had not occurred to me that knowledge itself could be ranked this way. I had been educated to believe that all knowledge, all learning, was intrinsically valuable, no matter that certain branches might lead to a greater professional income than others. All tended towards an understanding of existence, and the human place in it.

As we headed east, the dark smudge I had first seen on leaving Moritz grew until it looked like a good-sized storm. Below it was a spike that grew into a triangle. Eventually we passed through a series of copses, and the smudge, which Moira told me was the University, was lost to view. After a few hours, we crested a series of low ridges, and at last I saw the University.

Imagine a dark cone, grey and black and dismal, that as you approach resolves itself into a series of towers and spires, turrets and bridges, heaped up in crazy, gravity-defying columns, built almost one atop the other, of heavy stone. Around it fly what at first appear to be specks, which after another few hours of travel towards it appear to be crows, until the University is close enough for the traveller to realise that those motes, soaring and wheeling among the towers, are condors. The even tinier specks, just now visible, that the condors watch, are crows. Above it all, above the central, impossibly highest tower with its pointed slate roof and pennons, hangs a dark, black cloud, the grandfather of all thunderheads, that overshadowed everything and threw the University into eternal gloom.

I was a long time of staring at this impossible architecture with my mouth open, before I was able to turn to Moira. Watching me closely, she said, 'Did you see the base?'

I had not noticed the base. At the very bottom were high walls, and around the walls, a grey moat. I had never imagined a moat so wide. Access to the University was by way of a single bridge that pointed across the water at a dirty-looking little hamlet. Beyond the University, the moat stretched away to what looked like a wide expanse of mud and marshes. I caught the sound of breakers and smelled salt.

'A moat. And we are near a sea,' I said.

'No moat,' she replied. 'That is the sea. The University is built in the ocean.'

And so I came to the University.

ARRIVAL

It was late afternoon by the time we reached the narrow, rocky plain that skirted the bay. I had not realised the scale of the University before. It loomed over us, a dark and dank grey immensity, taller and greater than anything human-made that I had ever before seen or heard of. If it was built by humans. The condors wheeled overhead, and the sound of the wind as it passed between the towers was an unceasing, low moan.

The line of carriages wended its way along a track among the rocks, heading towards the bridge, which turned out to be a massive ornate affair of steel-sheathed timbers and burnished flat stone, connected to the University by steel hawsers that must have been as thick as my body. On the far side of the bridge, I could see, was a kind of open space below the grey-black walls. The walls were broken there by a series of gates. The grand entrance. On the near side of the bridge was a small hamlet, a sad affair of stones and mud and fish curing racks. Smoke rose from a few houses. A dog barked, dispiritedly.

'This is the village of Drab,' said Moira, tugging at my arm.

I could see why. We were passing through the middle of it now. Dogs barked with more interest, and a few thin children, filthy, followed the carriages at a distance. The village smelled of burning peat and drying fish and seaweed and poverty. From below, a few of the students broke into a song about class war.

'Many candidates wait here once they've sat the entrance examinations,' she continued.

'Here?' I could not believe.

She nodded. 'Sometimes it takes months for people to hear whether they have been accepted or not.' She lowered her head to my ear, as though to avoid eavesdroppers. 'It's said that the village was founded when one student waited so long that he took up fishing as a trade and got a wife. I think his application was lost but nobody notified him. So he just grew old out here and died, waiting.'

Moira brightened, 'Still, there's always a place at the University for people with money.'

My uneasiness grew as we left Drab and turned onto the bridge. By now the gloom of the dark clouds that circled the apex of the University had given way to the even murkier dark of the University's shadow. I suspected that whenever one was near or within the University, one would always be in its shadow. And the darkness within me, the heaviness in my chest, grew deeper.

How was I to get past the gate? I had little faith in my note, after Moira's opinion of it. I would try it, but I suspected that Strigge, whoever he may be, would simply laugh at me. Would an honest, but failed attempt to enter the University be enough for Finch? I doubted it. Well, if it didn't work, he was the ghost, not me. Perhaps he could pull a few supernatural strings.

We unloaded at the landing near the massive, ironshod gates. I wondered why a university needed the defences of a fortress.

Moira collected her few things and I untied Just Mule, watching the students climb out of the carriages as I did so. Many, perhaps the more drunken ones, had fallen asleep on the trip, and were now yawning and smacking themselves on the forehead to try to wake up properly. Porters came forward and took the students' luggage, for those that had brought any. One of the gates opened, and the students, laughing and punching each other on the shoulders, disappeared into the gloom, followed by the porters. The gates closed.

Then another, smaller gate opened at the end of the row, and the remaining people, employees, made their way towards it.

'Well,' said Moira, smiling at me as she gave Just Mule a stroke on the ear, 'this is where we part. I have to go through those doors and report. You should speak to Strigge.'

'Yes, thank you. But where is this Strigge?'

Moira pointed to a blank section of wall near the open servants' gate. 'Just there. Don't be fooled, there's a window there.'

Feeling a bit foolish, I walked over to the blank wall. Once I was close, I saw that there was, indeed, a camouflaged wooden shutter at chest height. I knocked on it. Silence. I knocked again, more loudly this time.

The shutter slid across. Behind it was a man at about my height. He was old and drawn, with a long white waxed moustache that stood out horizontally, away from his thin cheeks. His eyes were a milky blue.

'Yeah, yeah. I'm not deaf.' The man's voice crackled and sizzled and popped, like a spider on a hot plate.

'Excuse me,' I began, but he cut me off.

'We're closed. It's holiday. Come back in a year. A year. Closed.' He tried to slide the shutter closed, but I was already leaning on the counter and it stopped against my shoulder.

There was a pause, and he considered my bulk in his office window. 'Well, since you put it that way, what I can I do for you?'

'I'm looking for Strigge, I —' then he cut me off again.

'Ah, Strigge. Right, Strigge. You think Strigge is available for anyone who just sidles up to the counter? Hmm? Just sidles up?' The raspiness of his voice made my head hurt. Surely it hurt his throat to speak that way.

The person at the counter may well have been Strigge, for all I knew. In fact, it probably was Strigge. Well, no matter. He was being obstructive. I was a bureaucrat before I started on this fool's quest, and I know how to deal with such people. Without taking my eyes off him, I placed a silver coin on the counter between us.

The potential Strigge stopped clucking and looked down at the coin. He screwed up his face: slowly, his left eye and nostril closed to a point, while his right eye and nostril grew wider and wider. At the same time, his mouth wandered over into his right cheek, and the right corner of his mouth opened. The tip of a tongue, slightly blue, poked out. Then with his very wide eye fixed on the coin as though it would run away if he so much as blinked, he slowly lowered his head until eye and coin were separated only by his lashes.

'What's this?' he muttered. 'Very hard to see, hard to see.'

I pushed another coin next to the first.

'Ah yes. That's better. Yes.' He straightened up and looked at me again. The coins vanished under the blur of his moving hand. 'Now then, how can I help you?'

'I'm looking for a Mr Strigge. I understand he works here.'

The scratchy-voiced old man all but beamed his pleasure. He held his arms out, palms facing me, in an attitude of benediction. Then he brought his hands back to his chest as fists, rapping himself on the ribs to indicate, as I'd suspected, that he was Strigge. Nevertheless, it was a well-timed performance, or would have been, if punching himself in the ribs didn't bring on a bout of coughing that doubled him up for a couple of minutes. Just Mule jumped a little at the noise, which sounded like the world's biggest spider, on a hotplate, with bronchitis.

Eventually he resurfaced, looking a little shamefaced, but only a little.

'I take it you're Mr Strigge.'

'I am he, true. The one and only, the only and one. And it's just plain Strigge, no 'meestah' about it. I work for a living. Yes. Work.' He nodded, as though making a point.

'Well, Strigge, it's about work that I've come —' He cut me off.

'Work? Work?' He sucked his mouth in, as though drawing breath. Then his face seemed to disappear into the hole. It all exploded with a sigh, 'Work? There's no work here. None. No.'

I reached into my coat and pulled out the note from Cousin Imelda. 'I have a note, says here it's from Cousin Imelda.'

His face now with all the extremities back in their customary places, he snatched the proffered note, unfolded it, and placed it flat on the desk. He read it.

'Fake,' he said, his eyes still on the paper.

I was about to protest, when I realised what he meant. I placed a coin on the sheet. It disappeared, as did the note. Before I could demand it back, he went on.

'Although now that I look at it more closely, I see that it is in fact in dearest Cousin Imelda's charming hand. And how is she? Well, well?' here he glanced at me, but went on before I could speak. 'Yes, well I trust. Perhaps something is possible.'

He rubbed his chin, reached out from under the counter, and handed me a sheaf of papers.

'Application forms. Fill them out with a scribe.'

'Scribe?'

'Over there.' He nodded behind me. I glanced around, and saw a line of desks under a canvas awning, where presumably scribes could be hired to help compete the forms, but there was no one there now. I looked back at him.

'Closed now, yes. Gone home to eat fish. Come back tomorrow.'

Foolishly, I stepped away from the counter and Strigge, who never missed a trick, slammed it shut immediately.

Angrily, I rapped on the shutter. 'Closed!' came the muffled reply. I swore, but then remembered his motivation. I shook my purse, close to the shutter. It opened again. This time, I placed two large gold coins on the counter. Hie eyes widened, then he looked up at me. Very clearly, I said my name. He, with an expression that suggested he meant it, repeated: 'Shipton'. I stepped away from the shutter. He forgot to close it.

Then it occurred to me that I would have to spend the night in Drab, with Finch at my elbow. And with no real prospect that my bribes would get me in the University. The shadow in my heart darkened.

The carriages had already left, presumably on their way back to Moritz for the night. All but one. The driver sat atop, watching me. I walked over to him, leading Just Mule. The driver touched his hat with his whip.

'Hello,' I said.

'Hello to you,' he had an accent like mine. 'Can I give you a lift across to Drab? Seems to me you're wanting to come back here tomorrow.'

I thanked him, hitched Just Mule and climbed up next to him.

'Oh, it's no great suffering to wait for you,' he said, as the carriage turned around and then out onto the bridge. 'I live there. And your accent tells me we're countrymen.'

I told him what district of the city I came from, and he told me that he had grown up in the district opposite, on the far side of the canal. His name was Polk.

'Why are you here, Shipton, so far from home?' he asked me.

'I'm looking for work. Curious.'

He snorted, and wished me luck. 'I don't mean to laugh. I'm here to study. I sat the entrance examinations eight months ago. For the last six months I've been driving drunken scholars and tight-lipped workers back and forth from the University to Moritz.'

'Are there many like you?'

He turned to me. 'Many? Yes, and no.' He waved, indicating the village ahead, the bay, the rocky cliffs, the sky. 'Some live in Drab — some even give up and settle there — and others fish. There are hamlets all along the coast, you know, and hermits in caves. They're the really antisocial ones: they've come to study Sociology or Demography, or so I hear. Getting in can take days, or it can take months. Years.'

He paused, looked at his hands, the rein and whip. 'But I won't wait that long. If I don't hear anything by winter, I'll go. I don't need to study, there are other trades.'

'What do you want to study?' I asked.

'Natural history. You know, I want to know all about the movement of the stars and the moon. Always have.' He smiled.

We turned into Drab. 'Well, we're here!' he said.

I started to thank him, but he cut me off. 'Countryman, I live in Drab. I'm not going to Moritz tonight. Stay with me. There's beer and bread and a fire and smoked fish.'

Polk brought the carriage to a halt near a two-room cottage. Standing in the light of the open door was a young woman. She came forward, welcoming and smiling. Polk blew her a kiss and leapt down, throwing his arms around her.

'Sweetness!' he yelled, then kissed her on the cheek. I clambered down.

He introduced me as his guest, a countryman of his. The woman's name was Mary. I took her to be his wife.

'All the comforts,' smiled Polk, holding his arms wide to indicate the hut behind him. We untethered the horses and Just Mule and took them into a stable. Polk forked up some hay and a handful of oats for each animal, and then we went into the house. It was warm inside, a fire in the hearth throwing a slightly ruddy glow over everything. There was a pot of some sort of fish stew set over the fire, and on the table were mugs of beer. We sat down, and Mary helped Polk and me remove our boots, which she set to warm.

Polk smiled, looked at me, and then back to his woman. Here he was a different man. As a carriage-driver, Polk radiated a strangely ambivalent air, a mixture of determination and despair. He was determined to enter the University and undertake his studies, yet there was also fear that this was only a daydream and that his ambitions would not, after all, be realised. In this hut, that two-sided Polk disappeared: here, he was at his ease. Cares and ambition were left at the door and, clearly, Mary was the cause of that.

She was short, but with shapely hips and breasts. She had long dark hair and a shy smile that glowed when she chanced to look at Polk. She was a native of Drab, born and raised on fish stew and forever in the shadow of the University. She had a way about her, reserved and polite with me, to whom she never raised her eyes, but gentle and direct with Polk. For a moment I was reminded of Alexa, although Mary was utterly unlike her: perhaps it was the domesticity that made me think of my wife. The nostalgia was a blow to the stomach, and for a moment I had to hide behind my mug.

We ate Mary's stew, which was good, hot and filling, and then talked over beer until late. Polk explained that drivers usually ran two days on and one day off, staying a night in Moritz (on such nights he generally stayed with Mary's cousins, who were cobblers there). He and Mary had met shortly after he sat the entrance examinations. At the time, he had built a little shanty on the edge of Drab — as many did — and was still optimistic that he would soon be summoned to begin his studies. As he waited and the days passed, he watched every morning as the young women of Drab took their household laundry down to a rocky section of the shore to clean them in salt water. One woman in particular caught his eye, and without thinking too hard about what he was doing, he engaged her to wash what little laundry he had. Hands touched as clothes were passed, which led to looks, which led to smiles, which led to courtship. They were married not long after.

The family were not unhappy with the arrangement, especially as, being a potential student, he had prospects beyond the mud-shovelling life Mary could expect in Drab. In the meantime, they had helped him obtain the license for the carriage. The carriages and horses were actually owned by the Moritz municipality, and his wages were paid by them. The money was not great, but then, neither were their needs. When he said this, he and Mary had smiled at each other and squeezed their hands together. I envied him that smile.

According to Polk, while students were housed within the University, they were not permitted to bring spouses or other dependants. He and Mary had discussed this, and it was agreed that she would stay with her parents while he was studying at the University, although he would come away at intervals to be with her. It would be hard, but they knew it was for only a little time, a few years, and even at the worst, they would be separated only by some water, a few hundred metres at most. When he finished studying, he would become an academic at the University and then Mary could join him.

'But what about home?' I asked, meaning our city.

Polk stretched, weighing his words. 'I can't go back. You know they don't like people leaving.'

Like me, he could not go back.

I wished Mary and Polk well with a heart that wished nothing at all. The envy had grown as I sat and listened to Polk and watched them be in love. I stole glances at Mary, at her plump breasts that wanted a man's hand stroking them, at her throat white and ready to be kissed, at her exciting blushing cheeks. Her lashes were surprisingly long and langorous for a peasant girl.

Eventually, they turned in. Wishing me a healthful sleep, they went into the other room and drew the curtain. I rolled up my cloak for a pillow and lay down on the table, warm near the fire, trying not to think of hands and thighs and conjugal delights.

I had perhaps taken three breaths before I saw the familiar coat and leggings of my spectre. I looked up at Finch's face.

'Nice little thing, isn't she?' he asked, without preamble. Was he smiling or sneering? Hard to tell in the amber glow.

'Shh,' I whispered, 'they'll hear you!'

'Ah, no,' he said, his voice seeming loud. 'But they will hear you. Or have you forgotten the rules of the game? So be quiet and let me speak.'

He was right. Apart from the caravan master, nobody but me could see or hear the ghost. I shrugged, which he took as acquiescence.

'Excellent,' he began, 'a captive audience for once. No more chit-chat.'

'As I was saying,' he wandered to the fire, facing it. He raised one arm in the air, finger extended. 'As I was saying, that Mary is a sweet piece of meat, don't you think? The sight of her almost warmed my heart. I've been thinking, you know, that we're close now, very close. Perhaps you deserve a reward. Something to encourage you. And Mary seems like a nice, encouraging fillip, no?'

If he could have seen my face!

'I am not without influence, you know. I could arrange it. You could be sharing Mary's bed, rather than that fool of a husband. Hnf. If they let specimens like that into the University these days, then what are things coming to?'

Finch turned his back to the fire. He started, as though surprised, but it was only for effect. 'Oh, he's a countryman of yours, is he? Well, no one would guess, and that's to your advantage.'

I did not want to admit it to Finch, but I wanted Mary. I hadn't been with a woman in a long time. I could not imagine how a sneering, disembodied spirit with a dirty mind could possibly arrange to give me Mary and perhaps put Polk out of the picture, even if only for one night. It might be possible, but I was a guest among these people, and I would not take advantage of them.

'No,' I whispered, miserable and angry.

'What?' he cupped hand to ear in a theatrical gesture, 'I can't hear you.'

'No,' I whispered again, as loudly as I dared.

'Did you say "no"? My boy, friend Shipton, whatever shall we do with you? I'm offering you the little thing on a plate, and you turn me down? That's almost ingratitude, that is.' He chuckled.

I swore softly, to myself, and buried my head under my tricorn hat.

'Well, if that's the way it is, if you don't want to talk to me, then I'll leave.'

I don't think he did leave, but I kept my head hidden and refused to acknowledge his presence. Eventually, I dozed off. If there had been something important that he'd wanted to tell me, Finch lost his chance. And then I realised that, once again, I had forgotten to demand some answers. It was I who had missed a chance.

Next morning, Polk and I ate hot porridge with salt. He offered to take me back to the University. I thanked him, declining, saying that it was his day of rest. I was perfectly able to walk back over the bridge to Strigge. Besides, I had my mule with me, so I was not entirely alone.

He and Mary walked with me as far as the end of the village. It was always muddy, the shadow of the University ensuring that nothing dried out properly. Clothes had to be kept near fires or they became mouldy and fell apart. Children and dogs grew sickly, unless they were regularly taken away from the shadow, out into the fields and further up the coast, away from the mudflats. Many children

were sent for long visits with relatives elsewhere, either in Moritz or
the hamlets in the hinterland. This had happened to Mary, who
often, as a child, stayed with her cobbler cousins.

When we reached the end of the village Polk slapped me on
the back and wished me good luck. Mary handed me a loaf of
bread and some fish cake. I tried not to look at her.

'Remember, countryman, that if you're not admitted, you're
to come back. There's always a warm spot by the fire for you with
us!' Polk said, and I was glad to hear it. But I would not return,
under any circumstances: Finch would like that too much.

Polk looked over my shoulder, and I saw the contentment
dribble out of his eyes, replaced by the longing for a place in that
forbidding hulk. I followed his gaze to the towers of the University,
and set out.

After walking along the path for a time, I came to the
University bridge. From the carriage, I had not realised just how
huge this bridge was. It was built of timbers that could not have
come from any tree I had ever seen. Surely no tree ever grew that
thick? Stones the size of men. And all of it bolted and shod with
steel, the size of the pieces such that it took my breath away. What
travelled on this bridge, giants? Not for the first time, I was
astonished at the enormous scale of everything to do with the
University. As I walked, I pondered the skill and resources that
must have been engaged to build this. How long could it have
taken? And why in the middle of a bay?

Just Mule snorted, as though reading my thoughts and
echoing mine, agreeing that they were probably mad. 'They' in this
case included me.

As I approached the landing area near Strigge's office, I saw
that, despite the earliness of the day, it was already swarming with

people. There were a number who, dispirited and mudstained, had the air of would-be employees or hopeful students: those attempting to get in, or get information, or just get something, anything. Among them were others, dressed in a strange jet black, with shiny elbows and knees from wear, and jet black berets, who rushed about, clutching wads of paper or rolled-up tubes of documents. Here and there were vendors with panniers or little handcarts. Some seemed to be selling stationery or forms; others sold refreshments, fish crackers, fish broth, deep fried fish giblets. Or for a change, chickens' feet. Sometimes the dejected travellers followed one or another of the shiny-arsed, black-clad scarecrows at a distance, as though watching the movement of their own papers; sometimes they accosted the black ones and gesticulated wildly before the scarecrow ducked away. Several travellers were pulling out their hair or tearing up papers; one was seated on the stonework over the bay, perhaps considering tossing herself in. Further towards the great walls were the scribes' stalls, in a row, covered with canvas. Each had a queue of travellers leading to the stall, where a man or woman sat at a high desk, quill in hand, asking questions of whoever was at the front of their respective queue. Near each scribe there was always a scarecrow who watched every move the scribe made: at a certain nod or hand signal, the scarecrow would dash off into the crowd. Immediately, another scarecrow would take the first one's place, popping up from apparently nowhere. The whole area was filled with a seething and a bubbling, a rush of dreams and hopes crashing against a bureaucracy, too heavy and slow to even be cynical.

I tied Just Mule to a projection on the stonework and fed her a handful of oats. 'Wish me luck,' I said to her, and then dived into the swirl.

A scarecrow rushed past. I mumbled, 'Excuse me,' to get his attention but he didn't even notice, let alone stop. The second was no better. For the third, I stood in front of him, and when he tried to skirt past me, grabbed him by his black cravat, right close to the throat.

'Where do I get this filled out?' I yelled into his face, waving the forms that Strigge had given me.

'Glak,' he said, and waved towards the scribes. Which is what I'd thought, but those queues weren't moving very quickly. Then he tugged the cravat free and was off, gone in the crowd. So, steeling myself for a long wait, I joined what looked like a medium-sized queue. The short ones are always deceptive.

It took nearly three hours, but eventually I got the form filled out by a fat scribe who giggled and wore smoked glasses. Apparently the form was an application for employment. Many of these were filled out in a day, few were answered in a year, according to my scribe. Oh, he was a cheerful fellow! When it was complete, I made my mark and he affixed a seal. I paid him, and he told me that it now had to be lodged with the Office of Placements. Who? He waved airily. I should expect a request for further information in three to six weeks, I should return in that time, after lodging my form. Where was the Office of Placements? Again, he waved airily. And if the Office of Placements approved further action, my request would be sent to one of the Office of Temporary Employment, the Office of the Manager of the Register of Temporary Employment, the Department of Facilities, or Staff Registry. That was where things got confusing. I thanked the scribe, deciding to circumvent all this by dealing directly with Strigge. After all, I had paid a perfectly good bribe to him the day before.

I went over to Strigge's window. It was shut.

I knocked on it, loudly, not letting up until he yelled that he was not open.

Clearly, through the wood, I said my name. Almost reluctantly, the slide opened.

'Who?' he rasped, faced scrunched into a question-mark.

I repeated my name. Then I put down a silver coin. Quick, his hand passed over the coin, both disappearing back over the far side of the counter.

'Ah yes,' he said, nodding slowly, to himself. 'Shipton. You're from yest'y. So long ago.'

'I have a form.' I leant forward, placing the completed application in front of him.

'Office o' Placements,' he said, without even glancing at it. 'Yes, Office o' Placements.'

As I withdrew my hand, I dropped two gold coins onto the form.

Strigge's head lowered, until his eyes were next to the coins. He licked one.

'D'you know, this is a fine application. My, my, yes! A fine application. I think we should deal with this one straight away. Office o' Placements'll just slow it down. And the University needs go-getters like you. Yes.'

He folded the form so that the coins were safely inside it, and removed them both from the desk. Then he tilted his head slightly back, over his shoulder, all the while eyeing me, and bellowed, 'Strachey! Straaaah-aaaaaaaaachey! If you please!'

There was a strange stirring in the darkness behind Strigge, followed by a quavery little voice.

'Yes, Strigge?'

'There's a jennelmin —' that was how he pronounced 'gentleman' '— out here what needs to be sent to the Aardvark. Yes. Here's his papers, I want you to let him in!'

Just like that. Perhaps I hadn't even needed to have those forms filled out. Everyone has his price, and by patient accumulation I had found Strigge's. Now I was getting in.

I FIND A POSITION

If I had thought it gloomy outside, that was nothing to what it was like beyond Strigge's gate. It took my eyes a while to adjust. In front of me stood a tall, thin fellow with very thick, black eyebrows and a long, hooked nose. A drop hung from the point at the end of the nose, just about to fall, but never doing so. He held up a candle, and peered at me carefully. Lanky, but with a strange tension in his frame, as though it were not yet fully extended but might rapidly become so at any moment. He looked like the bastard child of a jack knife and a stick insect.

He coughed, and held up to his face the papers I'd had the scribe complete.

'You're, ahm, Mr Shipton.' I nodded. 'Very good,' he continued. 'Quite right.'

He paused, and considered Just Mule, who stood immediately behind me.

I looked around. I was in some sort of narrow antechamber, dim and walled of rough and wet-looking stone. I had expected the gates to open into a courtyard: perhaps the other gates, further along the wall, did. This, after all, was the workers' entrance.

At this point the jack knife cleared his throat and, placing my papers inside his waistcoat, offered me his hand. 'Well, I'm Strachey. Strigge asked me to take you to the Aardvark. Ahm. He'll sort you out, job and that, Mr Shipton.'

I thanked him. Behind Strachey was a corridor faced by doors on both sides. In a slight recess was a bench. Two children slept there.

'You there, child!' yelled Strachey, not unkindly. 'Up!'

One of the children stretched and yawned, looking at us confusedly.

'That's it!' said Strachey. 'Very good! Now, I want you to take the gentleman's mule to the stables. You c'n remember that?'

The child nodded. Before Just Mule was taken away, I lifted the smaller pair of saddlebags and draped them across my shoulder. Although most of my belongings were going off with the mule, I would at least retain my pistols in their box in the bags. I didn't like the idea of going about such a place completely unarmed. Polk had reminded me that only a very select few people in the world, those from my city, were my own kind. Everyone else was a stranger, and that included Finch. Especially that included Finch: he wasn't even alive. I was among strangers, and could rely only on myself.

The child was walking away when Strachey softly cursed, hit himself on the forehead, and called the child back.

'And what else?' he asked the child.

The child looked at him, then at me, then at Just Mule, and then back to Strachey. Its eyes widened, it shrugged, and then shook its head. It obviously had no idea what else.

Strachey hit himself on the head again. 'A receipt! Always get a receipt from the stables! And bring the receipt to this gentleman. He'll be with the Aardvark. Do you know where the Aardvark is?'

The child indicated that it did know where the Aardvark was. Strachey dismissed him or her with a wave.

'Now,' he said, turning back to me, candle cupped behind free hand, 'if you'll kindly follow me, Mr Shipton, I'll take you to the Aardvark.'

He set off down the corridor and, as I followed, I glanced up towards the ceiling. Way off, higher than I cared to think, I saw a narrow, irregularly-shaped rectangle of grey, ever so slightly lighter than the darkness that framed it. As I gaped at this, a dark shape, a dot, traversed the grey. And then I realised that I was staring at the overcast sky.

I had to hurry before I lost the human stick insect in the gloom.

How far did we travel, by what means did Strachey remember such an impossible route? Along corridors, up staircases, down ladders. Across great halls where sunlight seemed to filter through stained glass windows, picking out dust motes before alighting on weapons and armour obsolete centuries ago. And yet I knew there was never any sunlight here. Around a fountain that bubbled and burbled, populated only by swans and ducks, the fountain carved in the shape of the universe, with the motions of the planets and stars all captured and reflected, or so Strachey claimed. Once we went by rowboat down a flooded hall, where ruined paintings disappeared into muddy water and seemed to ask our help. Past a park on the roof of a building, where dogs chased balls thrown by women dressed as foxes. Sometimes it was light, sometimes dark. Sometimes there were smells of cooking, or sounds of revelry or a single voice, lecturing on some topic

I could not understand. Sometimes we travelled in silence, sometimes Strachey spoke, pointing out the work of a past chancellor or marechal. And then he spoke of the way things were.

'Remember, Mr Shipton,' he said, 'there's three kinds of people here. Ahm. There's the students, they's as what are here to learn. Now, the students are mostly pretty easy to deal with. They talk big, if you take my meaning, but they's just here to learn and drink. Here today, gone next year, as Strigge likes to say. They're supposed to wear brown robes except in their own chambers.

'Then there are the scholars, they's as here to teach, or maybe do research. Mostly, they dress in black, but some have to wear yellow or blue. Watch out for the ones in blue, Mr Shipton. Now, the scholars think they run the place. Ahm. Well, in some ways they do. But mostly they don't.

'And then, last of all, there's us. The workers. Servants, perhaps. But we runs the show, Mr Shipton. Ahm. You see, nothing happens without us.'

It was no more than I would have guessed. In any great house it was the servants who truly ran the place. Nothing goes into or out of a rich man's house but the servants know all about it and have first claim. They keep the accounts, prepare the food, clean the clothes: the wealthy owner might believe he or she makes the decisions, but it is the servants who present the range of options from which the master may choose.

'Mr Strachey, you mentioned the scholars dressed in blue.'

'Ahm,' he said, clearing his throat.

'Why should I watch out for them?'

Strachey stopped, turned, and holding the candle up, stared at my face, as though trying to read the answer to my question there. After a time he answered, 'There are three places you never want to go in the University, Mr Shipton. You never want to work in the kitchens, you never want to retrieve a book from the Library's inner circle, and you never want to go near the underlake.

'I don't know about any of them. Stayed away. I've never seen the first two. But I've seen the scholars dressed in blue, and they're responsible for the underlake. They're the judges, you see.'

I didn't see at all, and said so.

'Well,' he went on, clearly not relishing saying whatever it was he was about to say, 'It's the judges as feed the undermonster.'

'Undermonster?'

'They say,' he said, leaning close, 'that the undermonster lives at the bottom of the University, that it eats the dead. But that can't be true.'

'Who says that?'

Strachey pulled away, as though slapped. 'Why, but everybody says that! It's common knowledge.'

He turned on his heels and, picking up speed, shot into the darkness. Trotting behind, I thanked Strachey for his advice, pondering on the word 'undermonster'. I didn't have long to think about it, because shortly afterwards, we came to the office of the Aardvark.

It was a plain wooden door in a nondescript corridor. There was a sign on the door announcing a position and a name, but someone had crossed out this sign and replaced it with the words 'The Aardvark'. I wondered if this was an insult, a title or a name. Or a combination of all three.

Strachey knocked at the door. A voice ordered us to come in.

Inside, the room was well lit, with candles and a window that looked out on a quadrangle bordered by trees. Facing the door, a bald fellow wearing small round spectacles, so dirty as to be almost translucent, sat behind an enormous hardwood desk. There were some papers on the desk, pens and a letter opener. Behind him the walls were covered in filing cabinets, perhaps hundreds of drawers, each neatly labelled in a small hand that I could not read from the doorway.

The filing cabinet stretched to the left; around, over and below the window, and then behind another desk, where another man, about my age, sat at a much less impressive desk. There were a lot more papers on this desk.

'Well, come in,' said the bald man. 'It's freezing out there!' Actually, it was reasonably warm in both the corridor and office.

Strachey introduced me, 'Mr Aardvark, this gentleman, Mr Shipton, is sent to you by Strigge, with his compliments. He hopes you'll be able to find a placement for him at your convenience.'

The Aardvark, or Mr Aardvark, smiled broadly. 'Oh, did he? How excellent!' For a moment it seemed that he might clap with excitement.

'Ahm, I have his forms here,' continued Strachey. The Aardvark put out his hand and Strachey, stepping forward, placed them there.

'Thank you, thank you,' and the Aardvark waved Strachey away.

'Well,' he said, walking backwards out of the office and jerking away into the gloom, 'I guess I'll be going then.'

It seemed that the Aardvark could barely contain his glee. He tapped the papers with his spare hand, rolled them into a tube, scratched his chin with one end of the tube, licked that end, screwed the lot into a ball and tossed it over his shoulder. He hadn't so much as glanced at the contents. I wondered how much he would cost to bribe.

The Aardvark clapped his hands, once. 'Well,' he said, his smile growing, if anything, wider. 'Want a job, want a job? Hmm?'

He leapt backwards off his chair. Standing behind his desk, his chin barely cleared it. He walked around to the front, waving at a spot just in front of me. Quick, like a startled deer, the other man raced around and placed a step ladder at the place indicated. The Aardvark climbed it. When he had reached the top step, his eyes were slightly above mine. He clasped his hands behind his back and began to rock on the heels of his feet, back and forth, very quickly. Still smiling, still watching me intently. He hmmed and aahed to himself.

'Yes, hmm. A job, hmm. Ah. A position.' His smile disappeared. 'These are not so easy to come by. Oh, Strigge may have his ideas, but … but, he's not here, you see, at the coalface. Hmm.'

He climbed down and waved his arm at the window. The clerk jumped up, grabbed the step ladder and moved it to the window. The Aardvark climbed it with some dignity, his back to me, gazing out the window. He proceeded to rock back and forth again.

'No, no indeed, hmm,' he mused. I guessed his price was going up all the time.

There was silence for a while, broken from time to time by the Aardvark's hmming and the scratching of the clerk's pen. I was confident that I could bribe the man, it was just a matter of getting him to the desk.

The Aardvark stopped, as though he'd had a sudden thought. He looked at me over his shoulder and asked, 'Tell me, by chance, can you do … things?'

I had no idea what he meant by this, but decided that I had best go along with it.

'Yes,' I replied. 'Things, yes.'

His face exploded in smiles. He climbed off the step ladder and motioned, more forcefully, for the clerk to move it back opposite me.

He climbed up and again rocked on his heels, this time with such rapidity I thought he might topple over. His knees cracked loudly.

'Can you really? Can you do … things?'

For a moment I was certain he was joking, then realised he was serious.

'Yes,' I assured him, 'I can most certainly do … things.'

'Things! Hmm! Yes! He can do things! Peter!'

The man behind the desk sat up straight. 'Aardvark,' he replied.

'Get out the employment form. Ha, ha! This fellow can do things!' They both looked at me like some kind of miracle worker. Did people lose more of their sanity the longer they worked for the University? 'Oh, how we've been looking for someone like you!'

Peter the clerk pulled out a form, licked a pen, and prepared to write.

'Name?' asked the Aardvark. I opened my mouth to answer, but then saw that Peter was already writing something down.

Nodding, as though enormously pleased with my answer, the Aardvark asked, 'Age?'

Again, before I could answer, Peter began writing and the Aardvark cut me off with another question.

And so it went on. At each question, the clerk wrote something, what? An imaginary answer? The first thing that came into his head? Was there even ink in the pen? I couldn't very well see.

My attention wandered, and I gazed out of the grimy windows behind the clerk. The sky was dark and grey, and black birds wheeled, darker than the sky but curiously lighter than the stone of the buildings opposite. What, who were in those buildings? Just as with the room I was in, they were lit to counter the gloom that coated the University: a few odd candles, just enough, squintingly, to see by. From time to time someone moved past the windows, a vague, flitting shadow.

And then, after about an hour and a half of their questions and answers, the Aardvark and Peter stopped. The Aardvark waved at the air, then made a chopping motion. He was looking at me, a half-smile vaguely benign.

'Well,' he said. He climbed off his step ladder and waved vaguely at Peter. The clerk jumped up, rushed to the step ladder and carried it to near the door. He opened the door and smiled to me, bowing. The Aardvark climbed up the ladder and faced me. The meaning of the two of them lined up next to the open door was clear. I stood up to leave, wandering what it was I had done wrong: should I have paid more attention? I felt, obscurely, that I had failed.

'Well,' he said again, his hands clasped behind his back. 'Peter!' He tapped the clerk on the back of the head. Peter skipped past me, to the desk where he had completed the forms. He grabbed the sheaf of papers and, with another bow, handed them to me.

'We are so pleased to have you join the University staff,' smiled the Aardvark. 'Astonished, yes astonished we are at your skills and experience!'

I smiled and shrugged in what I hoped was a modest way. The pair of them were completely mad.

'Although I must say, in all fairness to the University,' he continued, 'that you are also very lucky! Yes! There is quite a waiting list for people who want to work here. Study here. Teach here. Quite a list. I should know, I keep it.'

He waved his arm again and my eyes followed the arc of one hand as it took in the filing cabinets, the files scattered about, his desk. Then I saw that the desk, the Aardvark's desk, was not entirely level: one leg was broken a few centimetres from its foot. To straighten it up, they had placed folders beneath the leg. From the dust piled on the folders, it seemed to me that they must have been lying there for years.

'Yes, and we will add you to the other, more venerable list, of University employees,' the Aardvark said. 'We consider that you would be most suitable as a personal secretary to a don. Yes, they often have need of people, capable people, who can do things. Just as you can do things.'

I smiled then, at the stupidity of it, but he took that to be a sign of self-deprecation, for he said: 'No! No need for modesty! Your record speaks for itself.

'Now, it happens that the deputy head of the Department of Information has need of a personal assistant. Her name is Margolis. Associate Professor Margolis. You are to take this —' Peter grabbed my papers away and thrust a sheet of heavy card into my hand '— to Professor Margolis. She will explain your duties.'

The Aardvark smiled broadly and clapped delightedly. How Peter got behind me, I don't know: he could move fast when he needed to. But suddenly I was propelled by his hands in the small of my back, out the door and into the corridor. As the door shut, the Aardvark yelled, 'Remember, Professor Margolis, Department of Information!'

And suddenly I was alone in a dark corridor. I leaned against the wall opposite the Aardvark's office door, collecting my wits.

After a while, I glanced at the card. It was blank. I turned it over. That face was blank too. I turned it back to the first side. Still blank. The idiots! My card of introduction to the professor must be in their office. And, it occurred to me, I had no idea of where I was, much less of how to find Margolis, although I assumed she would either be at the Department of Information or they would know how to find her.

For a moment I fumed, and then I opened the door.

The Aardvark and Peter were seated at their desks, scribbling away. The Aardvark glanced up.

'Can I help you?' he asked. His tone of voice, his face, demeanour, suggested that he had never seen me before.

'Um,' I said, suddenly off-balance, 'I was just in here a few moments ago. You gave me this ...' I held up the blank card.

The bald man and the clerk exchanged glances.

'If you say so,' said the Aardvark, non-committally. He looked again at the papers on his desk, pretending to read them.

'But it's blank!' I said, shoving it in his face.

The Aardvark flinched, then, holding his head back from me, focused on the card. 'Not blank,' he said. 'Closed.'

I opened and closed my mouth. 'Um?'

He pulled the card from me, held it at arm's length, squinting. Then he tapped it on the table and, with a sharp flick of his wrist, brought it to my face. Now it was twice the length, with writing. I made out the words 'Margolis' and 'appointment'. It had been folded shut all the time, sealed by some art I did not understand.

The Aardvark snapped his wrist in the other direction, and the card closed again. He handed it back, disdainfully.

'So you see, not blank. Distinctly un-blank, to my eyes,' the Aardvark eyed me, tapping a pencil against his chin with a thoughtful and unreassuring look. 'Hmm. And now, if you'll excuse me?' he motioned towards the papers on his desk. Peter snorted, as though stifling a laugh. The Aardvark looked down, dismissing me.

I turned for the door.

'No matter how many things a promising new employee can do,' said the Aardvark, 'there is always the — ah — possibility; yes, the possibility, that we have made an error in employing. Some tasks are that simple.'

I turned back to the Aardvark. His face was drawn, speculative and malevolent.

I got out of there as soon as I could and shut the door behind me. I turned back up the corridor and headed away. I had my card, I had my appointment: I need never see the Aardvark or his assistant again. Smiling, not paying attention, I turned at an intersection, went down a flight of stairs, down another corridor, across a hall, through an arch, past several more intersections and only stopped when I realised that I still had not the slightest idea how to find Margolis or the Department of Information. And then it occurred to me that I was lost.

THE LIBRARY

As far as I could, I retraced my steps. After the shock when I realised I was lost, there was nothing for it but to go back to the Aardvark and ask, or beg, if necessary, for a map or at least directions to the Department of Information. So I went back a ways, cursing myself for my stupidity. It was only after about a half an hour of walking that I admitted to myself that I did not remember my way back to the Aardvark. Not a single corridor or room looked familiar: somewhere along the way I had taken a wrong turn.

I sat down on a bench. I was in a largish room, carpeted and curtained, with a half-dozen arches leading off to what I assumed were corridors much like the one I had come down. The hangings were faded and tatty. If they had ever been decorated with scenes, it was not now possible to view them. There were niches for candles, but none were lit. Instead, one wall of the room, the side opposite me, opened out onto large bay windows. Through the dirty glass I saw that, as ever, it was a gloomy afternoon in the University. One window was open, and there was a slight breeze, cooling on my hot cheeks. I had not noticed that I was blushing, but I was: with anger or shame I couldn't tell.

Yes, a wrong turn. Somewhere, far back, I had gone astray. Having left my city, my family, Alexa's family, honour dictated that I die: I had held the flintlock in my hand, held it to my head, and feared to pull the trigger. Finch's deal was an escape from that, but he knows the depths of my cowardice and I feel no gratitude to him, only a steadily growing hate. I need to destroy the spectre.

And I will destroy him. I don't how to to kill ghosts, but it must be possible. Somewhere in all this University, among the learned people and their books, there will be a way. Someone will have done it. And I'll find out how.

Not by a musket ball to the face. Not by a stake through the heart. Not by poison. But there must be some way to kill a ghost.

Nor do I know where Just Mule has got to. I hoped it was being treated well; I would need it to leave.

Suddenly tired, I stood up. If I sat at that bench any longer I would sink into despair.

I walked over to the window. Facing a blank wall, it looked out on a narrow alley. Below me, about three floors down, laundry hung from lines zigzagging across the alley. I watched a fat woman, red faced and wearing a red handkerchief on her head, walk among the sheets and bloomers, a basket on her hip. She disappeared from sight.

What place had I found myself in? What world of gloom and shadows and dust and mildew? It was called the University, as though there were no other. But since coming here I had seen little in the way of learning or teaching. No students, no scholars: only a profusion of jumped-up and half-insane bureaucrats, playing their games and applying their arbitrary rules. Lost and stupid men and women who derived what pleasure they could from tormenting the lost and the hopeless.

Nothing was clean. There were no books, no lecture halls, no air of learnedness. Just miles of decaying corridors and dusty rooms. And never anybody. Always empty. Just me, alone with Alexa's memory and Finch's ghost. Perhaps even when alive he had been nothing more than a ghost.

'Or perhaps not,' said Finch, quite close to me.

I started. In my reverie, I had wandered out of the room and down a wide corridor. Ahead of me was a balcony that overlooked an open room. There was Finch, half in shadows, leaning against the balustrade. He was leaning so far forward that, if he had been flesh and blood, I could have tipped him over without much effort.

'Oh, Finch,' I murmured. 'What did you say?'

He sighed, straightened and looked at me. I couldn't see his face very well in this gloom.

'I asked if you were pleased to see me,' he spoke slowly, affecting an air of great, but slightly strained, patience. 'As you did not answer, I ventured to suggest that perhaps you were not. Pleased to see me, that is.'

I looked around the hall, anywhere but at Finch. 'Why shouldn't I be pleased to see you? After all, you're the only familiar face here.'

'Nice try, Shipton, but that is not the same as saying you're pleased to see me, is it?' Finch stepped forwards. Then another step. He raised his hands as though to cup my face. As he stepped forward, a bar of light fell across his face. It was white, whiter than I remembered. No doubting it now, he was a dead man. And his eyes! They blazed. That fire within him, the one that shone only out of his eyes, was fanning up. Perhaps he was being consumed from within. Perhaps it was killing him.

This place was burning him. His vengeance, his grievance — whatever it was — that thing that had kept him here after death; it was brighter now, hotter. The University was his fuel. Would it, eventually, burn him out? An incandescent ghost, a white hot ball of old anger and futile rage? If I could delay my part in his vengeance long enough, would he explode in sparks and leave me free? And what ashes would a ghost leave?

I looked away, over the balcony and down to the auditorium below.

'Ah,' said Finch. 'The Hausen Lecture Theatre. Doesn't look much used now. No matter. The University has its own rhythms, its own patterns. So much of it occurs on scales of space and time too great for individuals that we discern only a very small portion of it.'

We were both by now leaning on the balustrade, looking down. Immediately below us was a podium with a lecture-stand. Rows of wooden alcoves with desks stretched away into the gloom.

'Yes. The Hausen theatre. Once used, now no longer. Perhaps again, one day. I used to lecture here, you know.' Finch glanced at me, then looked down again at the rows, perhaps imagining it filled with students.

'I was admired, once. A promising scholar. I taught well.' He snorted. 'Do you know why this is called the Hausen Lecture Theatre?' I shook my head.

'Well,' Finch continued, 'it is named after Longman Hausen, an ancient and illustrious scholar. He lived three hundred years ago and taught in the Faculty of Extraneous Details, an area of serious intellectual inquiry that has been defunct for some time. Unnecessarily so, if you ask me — in case you are an utter clod, you will have noticed that the world is filled with extraneous details. Very little is pertinent, let alone germaine.

'In fact, one might go so far as to say that the world consists largely of extraneous details. Not quite solely so, but so nearly so as to make almost no difference, at least not in any way that would be formally mathematically demonstrable. It goes without saying, therefore — and although it goes without saying, I say it merely for the benefit of completeness of exegesis — as I said, it therefore is almost unsayable that, since the difference between the extraneous and the pertinent is non-measurable, it must be the case that everything is extraneous, effectively. Or at least for all practical purposes.

'And if everything is but an extraneous detail, it follows that serious inquiry into causal relationships can hardly be expected to bear intellectual fruit: a universe of pure extraneity can have no causality. At best, and in layman's terms, it's a mug's game. We can only hope to revel in the sheer interplay of detail, the seething kaleidoscopic mass of things that aren't particularly relevant to anything, least of all themselves.'

Finch waved one arm in a commanding gesture. In life, he must have been a very good lecturer: I was rapt, and I hadn't understood a word.

The ghost chuckled. 'Oh, it's heady stuff, all right. Problem is, it's mostly nonsense.' Finch looked at me sideways, with an expression I couldn't fathom. 'Forget it. I just quoted to you from the discipline's late period, its senescence. It was about to implode. This all happened a century ago.

'Now Hausen comes from a much earlier period in the study of extraneity and detail, before the discipline became decadent. He lectured here, right below us. And one day he gave a lecture of such importance that this hall was renamed in his honour.

'I don't know what the room was called before then. Presumably it had a name.'

The ghost was silent. It occurred to me that if he had lectured in the hall below us, he must know where we were. I was about to ask him for directions, or better yet, to lead me to the Department of Information, when he spoke again.

'I'm disappointed in you,' he said. 'And do you know why?'

A pause. Well, two could play at this game.

Finch sighed. 'Sometimes you are such a clod. Very well, if you don't want to hazard a guess —' he looked at me pointedly '— and I suppose you are quite certain that you don't want to hazard a guess, then I suppose I shall have to tell you.

'Very well. Why am I disappointed? Because you haven't asked me what Hausen's lecture was about.'

I hadn't realised I was holding my breath. I exhaled and, in spite of myself, it sounded like a sigh. Finch smirked.

'I do know what the lecture was about, you know,' he said.

Being reasonably certain that I couldn't outrun a ghost, I waved to him to continue.

Finch cleared his throat and began in his best pedagogic style: 'It's said that the gods, who know far more about what it is to be human than we humans, gave moral behaviour — morality, if you please — to us. We did not think it up for ourselves. Now the gods all say, and you ask any priest, that to own too many things, to come into the possession of everything, and yet to lose yourself, your own shadow, is the worst that can befall you. It is said that the hells were so full of people who tried to own the world at the expense of their shadows that a special hell was constructed for them. It was something the gods had not foreseen, that humans would be so acquisitive, so in love with things.

'It was this that Hausen lectured upon on that day. Apparently, to have been at that lecture, on that day, was to be changed forever. There was even talk of a new movement, Hausenism, but the man himself refused to have anything to do with it. I suspect he may have been embarrassed by all the fuss: apparently he was a brilliant lecturer, but he never again lectured like he lectured on that day.

'The lecture was not recorded, unfortunately. We don't even have his notes. They were destroyed in the Solstice Fire that burnt through several of the Library's archival rooms about fifty years before I was born.'

Finch rubbed his hands together. 'Well, that's the story. I never thought that I would one day stand looking down on an empty auditorium, at a University where no one remembers me, where I receive no adoring glances from young female undergraduates, nothing. I'm forgotten, I'm merely a shade. I'd like to meet Hausen now and ask him to explain to me how it is that I have lost the world, and now possess only my shadow. For that is all I am.'

For a moment I felt almost sorry for Finch.

He looked away, so that I could no longer see his face. 'You've done very well. Here we are, in the University. And you have found a position. That's excellent.'

Finch turned back to me and his mouth was like that of the varieties of insects that eat their prey alive.

'I must admit that I didn't really think you were particularly promising stuff when I saw you on the Isle of Goats,' he began, 'and I considered letting you kill yourself. But then it became clear that you probably didn't have the courage to pull the trigger …' he trailed off.

'You won't kill for yourself,' said Finch. 'But I think you will kill for me. In fact, I know it.'

I opened my mouth to object, thoughts of crookedness and gallows, but Finch raised a hand for silence. He motioned me away from the balustrade, to a dusty looking-glass hung on the wall nearby.

'Look,' he said.

I blew away some of the dust and looked into the glass. I saw two men, of similar height and build, standing side by side. Finch and Shipton.

'Do you see us?' Finch whispered.

'Yes,' I said. 'What of it?'

'Which is which?'

I half-turned to say something, then looked back. There were two men. One was Shipton, and one was Finch. I looked from one to the other and back again, but I couldn't tell them apart.

'What is this?' I stammered.

Finch ignored the question. 'Am I becoming you? Are you becoming me? Where is the line that divides us?'

The thought appalled me. 'You're standing on my right, so that must be you there, on that side.' I pointed to Finch's reflection.

'Am I standing on your right? And why did you need to deduce whose reflection was whose?'

With a wrench, I pulled away. Enough of games with mirrors and words. 'Finch, when will you tell me who I am to kill? And why — really why, not just because they annoyed you.'

Finch chuckled and rubbed his hands. 'All in good time. Soon. You'll know soon, Shipton. I promise.'

'That's all very well,' I said, 'But frankly I'm getting tired of travelling all over the countryside at your behest. I want more, Finch. And now.'

The shade pointed a finger straight up. I looked down, silent and ashamed.

'Later, I will tell you all. I promise.'

'Then at least tell me why this place is so deserted! Everybody I meet calls it a, no sorry, the University, but apart from a handful of demented clerks, I've seen nothing that even hints at this being a place of learning. A handful of dusty lecture halls aren't enough, frankly. My university had more life to it than this ruin!' I paused to catch my breath.

Finch raised his eyebrows. He turned on his heel and, waving at me to follow, stormed down the corridor. Scuttling, I followed as best I could: shades move faster than the living.

As we went along, I wondered why, yet again, I was obeying his commands so unhesitatingly. As soon as Finch commanded, I obeyed, no matter how much I promised myself that his strange dominion would end, that I would refuse service. And yet, with just a disdainful wave over his shoulder, he wiped away all my resolutions. I remembered the gallows hill and my determination to leave the caravan: yet I had been unable to even go down the hill. Had I convinced myself of the folly of leaving, or did Finch have a hand in that?

Noise began to intrude on my thoughts. At first it was like bees, far away. Rapidly it increased in volume, until I could no longer think easily. And still we went along this corridor, faster and faster. I was running now, hearing ahead the rushing of waters, the laughing of students, the hubbub of many.

The corridor ended at a T-intersection. To our left and right, a wide gallery ran straight into the distance. Opposite, the gallery opened into an open space and, far away, was another gallery, exactly like one on which we strode. High above were enormous chandeliers, blazing with light.

Below us was a wide boulevarde, with more candles and
lamps blazing. Along the edges, as far as I could make out, were
stalls selling books and food and stationery and beer. Criers cried,
news-pamphlets were distributed, dogs barked, trained parrots
cawed. And down the centre wandered or strolled or ran students,
unmistakeable in their brown robes, sometimes talking in groups,
sometimes reading. And among them moved the scholars. Looking
down and to the right, the boulevarde stretched off, disappearing
into the fog and smoke of so many lights. And to the left, was
a wide flight of steps leading up to an arched entryway, singing
with light. Above the arch was the single word, 'Library'. I gasped.

Finch looked down with a complacent air.

'Welcome, at long last, to the University.' He spoke with
quiet smugness. He enjoyed overawing me, his pet bumpkin. 'This
is the North Boulevarde. At one end, as you can see, is the Library.
At the other, as you can't see, is the central quadrangle, the Quad.
Most people are in the Quad. It's pretty quiet down there — much
noisier in my day, I'm afraid.'

For a moment I couldn't speak. I had never seen so many
people together in the same place at one time, and all I could do
was watch them, the people walking, or talking or standing at the
stalls. Here and there were raised platforms, islands among the
general movement of people. On the platforms students lounged
or read by the light of smokey lamps, or sat in circles, smoking
pipes and talking.

As I watched, I began to see patterns, swirls of motion, some
faster and some slower, like the whorls and eddies of smoke in nearly
— but not quite — motionless air. There were secret currents to the
group, plays of movement, of which the individuals themselves
could not possibly be aware. It was only because I was so much

higher than they, and watching quietly, that I saw. Not only did I see the patterns, but I saw also that they had no significance at all. Perhaps this is the way of all human life, that it is a dance of patterns, all but invisible to the participants, who go about their business for days and years without once guessing that their individual being counts for nought, that they are merely particles in a swirl of pattern. And that this pattern is itself utterly meaningless, that it is of no more moment than the sudden change in direction of a scampering flock of sheep, or the dance of seeds from a dandelion.

I looked up. Not entirely to my surprise, Finch had gone.

I dusted my hands. It seemed that I had several choices: as I was at the Library, I could ask directions to the Department of Information and, therefore, hopefully find this Margolis person. Better yet, I might meet Moira on the pretext of asking her directions to the Department. Or I could give up on this stupid quest of revenge, somehow find Just Mule and make my escape from the University. If I was to walk alone among so many strangers, I would not do so unarmed: carefully, I removed the pistols from their case and stuck them in my belt.

A little further on from where I stood was an alcove containing the mouth of a spiral staircase. I headed over and began the long climb down to the boulevarde.

As the steps wound down, the noise grew. And so did the smell: the dust and mildew gave way to frying bacon and onions, tobacco, urine and the sweat of so many unwashed undergraduate bodies. At the foot of the stairs I stared down an alley between two rows of stalls, out to the human traffic beyond. To my relief, the cluster of bodies was not as dense as it had appeared from above. I took a deep breath and dived in, my hands resting against my pistols and purse.

As I walked, I overheard snatches of conversation: sales
pitches, seductions, philosophical arguments, questions on natural
science, challenges to duels, protestations of love or contempt,
discourses on politics, debates on horticulture.

The noise petered out as I reached the steps of the Library.
Hardly daring to look up, I mounted the steps, the light from
beyond the arches growing in intensity all the while.

And as I passed beneath the arches, the noises from the
boulevarde dropped away completely. I was in the foyer of the
Library. It was brilliantly lit, and very quiet. The Library building
was an enormous circle: stretching away to both sides of me were
rows of desks abutting shelves filled with books, the shelves higher
than three men standing on each other's shoulders. Students sat
here and there at the desks, reading. The shelves formed the
circumference of the circle. Directly in front of me, across a small
open space, was a large-ish closed-in area with a glass wall. Inside
were three people. I guessed this was the loans desk. Beyond that,
for as far as could be seen, row upon row of shelves, each taller than
a man, and stuffed with books, stretched into the distance.
I suspected that the Library was literally a circle, and so I should
have been able to see the far wall; however, it was too wide in
diameter for me to see that far.

I walked to the loans desk. Hanging from the ceiling by two
long chains was a sign, 'Outermost circle: reference section' and
below that, 'Shhh!'. A little awed, I made my way to the woman
who sat at the desk, reading.

I didn't quite dare break the near-silence by speaking, so
I waved to her. No effect. I waved again, this time a little more
vigorously. Her book must have been engrossing. Frustrated, I snapped
my fingers while waving so hard I thought my wrist might come off.

Immediately, she looked up. Her finger shot to her lips in that gesture practised by librarians everywhere. I was instantly sorry for all the times I had ever made noise, and not just in libraries. I was sorry for the very existence of sound.

'Can I help you?' she asked, in a tone that suggested she rather hoped she couldn't.

I didn't want to actually vocalise and decided to whisper, 'I am looking for a librarian …'

Ignoring my question, she looked me up and down. Finally, she said, 'You're not a student, are you?'

'Well, no,' I whispered.

'… Nor a scholar. Hmm. What are you?'

Perhaps she couldn't hear me whispering. 'I am a new employee of the University. Can you help me? I'm looking for a librarian.'

She straightened up. 'I am a librarian,' she said, accenting the 'I'.

'Yes. Yes. But I'm looking for a different librarian.'

'What's wrong with me?'

I was beginning to suspect that this conversation was a quagmire from which I would never escape. 'Is there someone else I can talk to?'

She looked around, stared hard at the other two librarians at the back of the loans area as if their presence there was a surprise to her, and then looked back at me. 'No; no one else, I'm afraid.'

Idly, I wondered if my pistols were loaded. I couldn't remember. Now might be the time to use one:

'Forgive me if I was not clear about exactly what I meant a moment ago,' I said, trying to keep my voice level. 'I am looking for a librarian who works in a different part of the library.'

'Oh! Oh! Well, why didn't you say so? Young man, you are terribly obtuse, you know. That is not an endearing characteristic in one so unformed.' She stood up. 'And where is this other librarian?'

I paused. Where exactly did Moira say she worked?

'The Circle of Natural History,' I blurted. And perhaps that was right.

'Ah,' she said, suggesting that she thought as much. 'Well, you understand the Circle of Natural History is one of the outermost circles. It used to be the outermost circle, but has just now been promoted to second-most outermost circle, if I can put it that way. Swapped with the Humanities. Literature, history, that sort of thing.'

She stood up from her desk and came out through a half-door, speaking as she went. 'That is to say, the Reference and Loans sections actually occupy the true outermost circle of the Library, in a merely geographical or architectural sense. But these areas are not actual disciplines, as it were; they are instruments of the Library. Of course, there are serious epistemological issues surrounding the construction and use of dictionaries and thesauruses, for instance.'

Once again, I had found myself in a conversation in which I understood many — although not all — of the words used by the other person, while the order of presentation of those words rendered the whole thing gibberish.

Thankfully, the librarian seemed to have reached what was, to her, a logical point to end the sentence. She cast a birdlike eye over me. 'Young man, there are a large number of librarians employed down there,' she waved in the direction of a stack of books. 'Do you have a name for this person?'

'Moira?'

She snorted daintily. Clearly the name meant nothing to her. 'Very well, head towards the centre of this circle' — again she waved towards a stack of books — 'there are a number of porters among the stacks, so if you get lost, just ask directions.

'Once you reach the centre, you'll see the great staircase. Can't be mistaken. Go down two levels. Two. That will take you to the Circle of Natural History. Expect there to be some confusion, young man: it and the Circle of the Humanities have only recently swapped places, so there will be lots of people reorganising, reshelving books, organising offices. Many will not have heard of the change, or will not have heard correctly. Don't listen to them, they don't understand that the Circle of Natural History is rightfully of higher precedence than the Circle of the Humanities.'

Once again, she waved vaguely in the direction of piles of books. 'That way. Now good day, I have work to do.'

I thanked her and, not at all confident, headed towards what I hoped was the centre of this circle.

Although the Library was comparatively well-lit, the spaces between the tall shelves of books was still gloomy. Spine after spine on the shelves, many in languages I didn't recognise. All reference works: dictionaries, thesauruses, encyclopaedias. So many words to define other words! I wondered if, somewhere, there was a dictionary of dictionaries, a central index. Who would compile such a thing?

After a time, I passed an old man sitting motionless on a stool, itself set in an alcove within one of the great stone pillars that supported the arched roof, so far above. Since he was the first person I had seen for a while, I stopped and nodded.

'Is this the way to the central staircase?' I asked.

He held out a cup and rattled it. It made the sound of two buttons hitting a penny. I dropped a coin in; porters have to eat, too.

The old man cleared his throat. 'Yus. Keep going as you are.'

I kept on. And on. Later, the way ahead became lighter, as though I was coming to the end of the bookshelf-tunnel. Within a few minutes the end was in sight. I came to an open area which, after the almost subterranean gloom of the shelves, seemed almost agoraphobic. I was at the centre of the circle. In front of me was a huge hole, perhaps nine metres in diameter. A double spiral staircase led down into the hole, which was ringed by a low stone balustrade and an assortment of reading desks. There were a few students here and there, as well as the odd librarian and two porters who were both seated on high stools at either entrance to the staircase.

I took a few steps forward and, happening to glance away to my right, saw a wide passage that led away from the staircase, into the forest of shelves. A trickle of students and scholars were walking along here. This must be the main access from the Library entrance to the main staircase. So why hadn't I seen it on the way in? And why hadn't the librarian I spoke to pointed it out to me? Perhaps that was why her wave was so vague: she thought the passage to be so obvious as to merit no special explanation and I, like a literal-minded fool, had headed directly towards where I thought she was pointing.

None of which was helping me find Moira. With a mental shrug, I headed towards the stairs, and down I went. At the next level, the traffic on the staircase suddenly increased. Hooded librarians moved about, going down the stairs or coming from below, and then disappearing into the rows of shelves that once again radiated away from the staircase. All were carrying piles of books or bundles of papers. Some were laden with crates on their backs, from which a book or two would occasionally fall, others had wheelbarrows full of tomes. A constant toil that made me think of ants. Books were pulled from shelves and taken down, others were put on the shelves in their place. I saw one hooded figure staring intently at the side of a shelf, until I realised he or she was trying to make sense of the accession numbers written there: would these be the old ones, or the new ones? Two circles were changing places and so their books had to move. Chaos!

There seemed no organisation to this, no guiding hand. As I watched, a student tried to remove a book from a shelf, presumably to read it. A librarian smacked their hand away with a length of birch and then, joined by two or three others, chased the student away, deeper into the shelves. Books were placed on shelves, only to be removed moments later by a different librarian and taken … where? To another shelf on the same circle, or back to the circle from whence they had come?

I joined the stream, passing this circle for the next one, the Circle of Natural History. Around me, librarians jostled, elbowing and muttering darkly at one another. At the edges, students and scholars inched up or down the stairs, hunched down in order to make themselves as inconspicuous as possible. We all sensed an ugly mood to the librarians, and anything might set them off.

At last I reached the next circle. This, presumably, was for natural history. The stream of librarians diverted from the staircase at this point. The few others on the staircase kept going, their relief apparent in the way they straightened their backs.

Things were no better here. It occurred to me, too late, that if Moira was here, she was almost certainly helping to reorganise the shelves. There was no chance of finding her without help, and I did not feel comfortable at the thought of asking someone.

Away to my left, I heard hissing. Two librarians were both pulling at a human skull, as though it were a rope in a tug-of-war. The argument between them was fierce; the hissing was the two of them interjecting in angry whispers. Suddenly, I realised that in all this chaos and repressed anger, everything, even the oaths of librarians who dropped heavy books on their toes, had been conducted as close to library-level quietness as possible. It was uncanny.

'No!' the first one hissed. 'No! You can't have it!'

'It's a skull! It belongs in natural history!' The second.

'It's not a sheep, you idiot!'

'Don't call me a sheep! I know it's not an idiot! By the Treaty of Quincieme, all skulls, bones and carapaces belong to the Circle of Natural History!'

'This isn't just some skull. This is the head of the Venerable Grymme and it belongs to the humanities!'

'Natural history!'

'No! This skull has inspired students for a hundred years!'

'It belongs to natural history, I tell you!'

'No! It's a sacred relic!'

'It's a bloody skull and you people have been holding out on us!'

One of them managed to pull the skull free. Quick, he spun around, swinging it into the other librarian's face. The skull, which must have been very old, shattered and the hapless librarian collapsed, blood and mucus spraying from his broken nose. Activity before this had been quiet; now, however, a silence, dark and ominous as thunderclouds, spread in a wave from the epicentre of the broken skull.

The librarian, clutching a forgotten bit of cranium in his hand, had just enough time to say, 'But …'

And then all the pent-up frustration and anger erupted.

I was surprised at the time by how fast I could move when I needed to: I'd never needed to before. Fists were swung, books rained down on noggins, people were stabbed with pens and pelted with rubber stamps. Blood, ink and library cards were spilled. I took off down the first aisle of half-empty shelves I could find, trying to get as much distance as possible between myself and the spreading battle. Whoever the Venerable Grymme had been, he was now just a half a cranium and the trigger of a riot.

I turned a corner and a librarian stepped out of the shadows. He swung a leatherbound volume at my head. Somehow I ducked back before it connected with my head and then one of my pistols was in my hand, the muzzle pointed square in the librarian's face. With a prayer to my ancestors, I squeezed the trigger.

Nothing happened. He looked at the flintlock. I looked at the flintlock. I hadn't loaded it! Again, I was surprised at how fast I can move. I took the heavy weapon in both hands, raised it over my head and, jumping forward, bashed him in the face with the muzzle. He grunted something and fell over. I kept running.

I ran further, deeper into the shelves. After a while, the number of books on the shelves began to thin until very few of the shelves held any books. I stopped running.

'Hey!' somebody stage-whispered. I looked around, empty pistol ready as a club.

'Up here!' I looked up. Above me, on the shelves beyond head height, lay perhaps a half-dozen people. They were mainly students, but there was also a porter and a scholar, judging from the colour of their robes.

'You need to get up here,' hissed the scholar. 'It's not safe in the aisles, they might see you.'

A couple of students grabbed me by the arms and pulled me up to safety.

I thanked them all. 'Are we really safe up here?'

'Yes, for a while,' answered the scholar, whose name was Vance. 'They tend not to look up. Kick the books away, if you have to.'

I looked around and saw people sitting on shelves at our height on row after row.

'Does this happen often?' I asked.

Vance shrugged. 'Often enough. They reorganise the circles every so often, and that's the most likely trigger for a librarian's riot. But really, they just need to get it out of their system every now and again. It's a venting of spleen.'

'One of them tried to brain me.'

'Oh yeah. They'll kill you if they catch you. At first they fight each other, then they'll blame it on the "outsiders", by which they mean any non-librarians. Then it's torches and pitchforks, and the hunt is on us, people who neither understand nor care abut the Dewey Decimal system. Not even the poor old porters are safe,' he nodded to the porter who shared our shelf, 'and the porters work here. They're as liable to lynching as any of us.'

This seemed a good time to load my pistols.

A short time ago, a mob of librarians rushed past our hiding place. They were carrying knives and staves and torches, howling and yelling. They clearly wanted blood, but couldn't see us in the gloom. We, however, could see them perfectly. I held my pistols at the ready, prepared to shoot.

Fortunately, they didn't stop, and after a few minutes, the group passed. But not before I saw Moira. Too intent on my own skin, I had not given her a thought since the trouble began. I needn't have worried: she could obviously take care of herself, a librarian among librarians. Whatever madness possessed them, it had carried her along. She stormed with the rest, a fist clenched in the air and a knife in her other hand. Her eyes were enormous saucers and she howled like a dog. Her robe was open at the waist and I saw, thrilled for a moment, her breasts. There was blood on her face and breasts — and it was not hers: it had been daubed on in patterns. I couldn't see the patterns very well in the torchlight, but could see well enough to know that she or someone else had fingerpainted in blood.

Had she killed? Been at the kill?

The mob passed and I no longer doubted that we are all monsters.

Somebody squeezed my shoulder. I started from my reverie to see Vance and the porter, Smith, looking at me with concern.

'We'll get out of here, you know,' said Vance.

I had been crying. They must have assumed I was crying with fear, but it was really in sorrow for myself and for others. But especially for Moira, lost to me. She might have been as dead as Alexa. I would never see her again: I could not bare to face her.

I nodded. 'We have my pistols, if there's need,' I said.

Vance squeezed my shoulder, then let go. 'Good man,' he said. 'I've been speaking with Smith here, and it seems there might be a way out. It's been pretty quiet for a few hours now. Either it's burnt itself out, or they've spread out to the other levels of the library. Either way, I don't want to risk running into them.'

Smith grunted. 'The librarians'll be goin' up and down the main staircase, so that's no use, but there are other ways around the Library.'

Vance cut in. 'Smith here tells me there are a series of access stairways at intervals around the Library's circumference. They all lead up and away from the building. So, if we can reach the nearest one ...'

Things had been quiet for some time, and there seemed little point in waiting, so we decided to make the attempt straight away. I had the only pistols and was not going to part with either of them, so it was agreed that I would go ahead with Smith, who knew the way. Vance and one of the burlier students would bring up the rear, with the other students between us. One student, too frightened or stubborn for his own good, refused to go. Nothing to do but leave him there.

Carefully, as quietly as possible, we lowered ourselves to the floor. There must have been torches or lanterns somewhere nearby, because we were not in complete darkness, although not far from it. I had little faith in old Smith's ability to navigate under these conditions, but decided to keep my mouth shut.

Through the darkness we crept, I with a pistol in one hand and the other stuck through my belt. Past great shapes that towered above us, seeming ready to collapse, that afterwards I realised were only book stacks. Twice we saw things huddled on the ground, things that may have been bodies. We did not stop to investigate. Occasionally we passed others like ourselves, refugees huddled on the top shelves. Sometimes they joined us, sometimes they did not. Each took their own chances. Sometimes we heard other groups creeping around in the darkness. We assumed these groups were also seeking the access stairways, but opted to not make contact in case they turned out to be librarians.

I don't know how long we half-shuffled, half-tiptoed through that dusty, musty, smoky gloom. At least a lifetime, certainly several hours. The strain was immense, and I began to stumble occasionally. I was not the only one. We had to stop and rest. Some nearby shelves looked like the safest place, so we clambered up.

'Close now,' said Smith.

'How close?' asked one of the students.

Smith considered. 'Half hour's walk, maybe.'

I was too tired to speak. I may have dozed. Too soon, Smith crawled off the shelf, tugging at my ankle as he went over the edge. I pulled myself up and, offering a prayer to my ancestors, followed him down.

We worked our way forward in the darkness. What little light there had been before was now almost gone. In order to stay together, we walked single file, each person holding the shoulder of the one ahead. Since Smith led, I was second in the chain. Onwards we went, and then without warning I walked into him. The student behind walked into me, and the chain folded on itself.

'What?' I whispered to Smith.

'The door. It's here.' He whispered back. I repeated this to the student behind me, and heard the news being passed along, whisper to whisper.

I don't know whether Smith used a key to open the door or whether it was unlocked. After a moment, there was a sliver of light ahead. Then it widened as Smith opened the door a fraction more. A little more and there was enough room for me to stick my head in over his shoulder.

It opened onto a landing. A four-sided staircase spiralled up and down, light filtering in from somewhere above.

'It seems quiet enough,' I murmured. Smith nodded, and went in.

We crowded onto the landing, Vance closing the door behind us.

'Upwards?' he asked Smith, more for confirmation than anything. The way was obvious.

'Aye,' nodded Smith. He started up the stairs, then stopped. I was right behind him, and I saw quite clearly the hairs on the back of his neck stand up. I had almost phrased the question before I heard, from above, a murmur. That murmur became a mutter, that became a shout, that was an oath, a door being torn off its hinges. Howling, torchlight, yells, a scream.

'Oh no,' somebody behind me moaned.

From above us, a student plummetted, screaming, down the stairwell. The scream went on for a long time.

'Down! We have to go down!' somebody yelled. And ahead of us, the mob got suddenly louder. It knew where we were.

I turned, and ran down the stairs. Out of the corner of my eye I saw someone bolt back the way we'd come, into the Library. Stupid — that place was a death trap. Heedless, sweat stinging my eyes, I took the steps two and three at a time, risking a sprained ankle with every leap. Someone, behind and above me, yelled for help; a yell that was cut off. And still I could hear the hopeless scream of that falling student. How far was there to fall?

Around and behind me others ran while above we heard violence, death, insanity. I lost track of time and did nothing but run down those stairs, forever and forever running, until

I couldn't run any more and only staggered on, leaning against the handrail, one stumble away from flipping over and following that student on a fall that would go on forever. On I went, terrified. And then I realised there was no noise of pursuit, no imminent death. We, all of us, had run, fallen, clambered, staggered on, long after our pursuers had ceased to follow. Perhaps they no longer burned for our blood; perhaps they thought they had caught and killed us all.

We lay on the steps or leaned against the banister, panting. Somehow, I still held onto my pistol. I stuffed it into the belt with its companion, my hands shaking, and fell to the ground next to Vance.

After we had caught our breath enough to speak, he asked me, 'Do you know where we are?'

I shook my head. 'Somewhere deep in the Library.'

He nodded. 'Near to the inner circles, I think.'

'Do you think they've stopped?'

'For now, perhaps.' He coughed and then wheezed. 'I'm a scholar, not an athlete.'

I looked around. There were perhaps half as many as had reached the staircase. I couldn't see Smith. Poor man.

'Smith's gone,' I said.

Vance looked around in the half light. He sighed. 'I hope it was quick.'

I checked my pistols. 'How are we to get out of here?' I asked. With Smith gone, Vance seemed the most reliable potential leader. I had no hope of escaping from the Library if I were alone.

Without looking up, I spoke. 'I'm a stranger here. I don't know where I am or where I'm going. What do you suggest? How do we escape?'

Vance thought for a while. 'It's strange. I teach literature. I don't have much idea as to where we are, or where to go from here. I do not think that we can go back, up there.' He shuddered.

'But then,' he continued, 'I don't know what lies below us. Perhaps there's no way out, that way. The only other possibility is that we go back into the Library. Find a door near here, go back in, and take our chances with the librarians.

'We must be near the lower circles of the Library. I've never been there, can't imagine what it's like. But I'd rather try that than go back.' He glanced up.

One of the students piped up. 'But how do we know that the librarians aren't rioting down here, too?'

Vance looked at the speaker. 'We don't know. Can't know. But what are our options?'

'We could wait,' the student suggested.

'How long? And for what? Help? Help won't come. But we may meet the librarians again. No, I think go back in.'

It struck me that re-entering the Library was a sure way of running into more librarians, not fewer. But I saw his point that we couldn't just stay where we were.

'Look,' I said, 'I think we all agree that we can't go up the stairs. And staying here is simply asking for trouble. But I'm not so sure that going back into the Library is the safest course. We've just escaped from there. Surely there are other alternatives?'

There was silence. Eventually, Vance spoke. 'As you say, you're a stranger to the University, that much is clear. If you were not, you would know that we would far prefer not to go down.' Around him, the students murmured assent.

'Why?'

'Because we don't know how far down the staircase goes. And things live down there, beneath the University.'

'What things?'

They stared as if I was mad.

'That's the way to the underlake,' said Vance. 'There are things in the underlake.'

I snorted. 'You talk of "things", things that you've never seen. I saw people killed by librarians today. Those librarians are above us, and in there.' I pointed at the walls. 'They are real. We know they will kill us if they get a chance.'

The students muttered to each other. I was speaking sense, but they weren't interested. It was obvious what the consensus was: we were going back into the Library, into certain death. If not bodily death, like Smith, then moral death, like Moira. I knew I could not continue down on my own, I would have to go where the group went. For a moment I thought about pulling my pistols on them and forcing them — but I am a lousy shot and, even if I were a marksman, not certain I could shoot someone in cold blood.

Vance held his hands out to me, palms upwards. 'I'm sorry, but we'd all rather prefer the Library route.'

I shrugged.

He stood up, and we followed him. There was no door here. We went down about two more flights until we came to another landing. There was a door here and Vance stood to open it. I came up on one side, both pistols drawn. There was a thrill in my belly at the thought of impending danger, of not knowing what was beyond that door. The academic turned the handle. He pulled. Nothing. He pushed. Nothing.

'It's locked,' he hissed.

'It can't be,' said one of the students.

'Well, it is.'

Vance let go with an oath. He moved away to the balustrade, and leant against it, looking down into the darkness. Although there were probably enough of us to batter the door down, that was clearly too dangerous: any noise might bring the librarians down on us.

'All right,' he said, 'all right. Can't open this door, perhaps the next one is unlocked. We go on.'

Downwards we went, several flights of stairs. And then we came to the next landing, the next door. It, too, was locked.

It's a strange thing that, although Vance and the students flatly refused to go to the bottom of the staircase and seek an exit there, they were happy enough to go down flight after flight, seeking an unlocked door. It didn't seem to occur to any of them to go up the stairs in order to find an exit, one that would be closer to the surface. Perhaps the knowledge that there were packs of librarians above them, while there was also a possiblity of no librarians below them, created sufficient force to impel them in that direction.

All I can say is that, landing by landing, door by door, flight by flight, over time, we gradually ran out of options.

The staircase ran out in a smallish open space. It smelled of old must and fresh blood: the student they'd thrown over the railings had come to rest at the bottom, his head crushed like an egg. Otherwise, there was not much else: some rubbish in one corner, a broom, and a door. The door was locked; however, the hinges had rusted to the point where it had simply fallen away, and was now hanging outwards, suspended by the lock mechanism alone.

Vance leaned forwards, straining to see into the darkness beyond the broken door.

'Pooh!' he whispered. 'It smells of old books. And dark.'

He pulled away, and facing us, made a fist and rubbed it in his other hand. 'I don't much like it, but I think it's the only way out.'

'How deep are we?' asked one of the students.

'Not that deep, I don't think,' Vance replied. The students relaxed at this. Were they concerned about Vance's 'things'? Did the things exist somewhere deeper still within the University? How far down did it go? Just as the place stood impossibly tall, its towers spindles, so too it seemed to plunge far into the earth. But weren't we in a bay? If we were underground, as I suspected we were, then this whole area should have been waterlogged, if not actually flooded. Yet everything was dry.

Vance leaned near the door, pulling at it. 'Help me,' he said, and two students pulled with him. The door came away from the lock, scattering dust and rust flakes. As it did so, the dry and dusty smell rose up, intensifying until it had a force not unlike a strong, foul-smelling wind. It smelled of old books, even more overpowering here than in the Library. Despite the danger, I couldn't stop myself: I sneezed and coughed simultaneously, a catch in my throat. My eyes watered and I sniffled. Two students who started to tell me to be quiet came down with their own choking, sneezing fits.

Then I was dazzled. Blinking, I saw that Vance was holding a torch. I'd been so long in deep gloom that it hurt my eyes.

'There's a box of them just near the door,' he said, waving vaguely past the doorway.

After we'd recovered from our coughing, we were handed lit torches. Light at last!

Past the door there were piles upon piles of books. The stacks, some leaning at crazy angles, vaulted up into the darkness beyond the range of our torches. There were mounds of books leaning against the piles, and small drifts of books collected in the odd corners of this geometry. Shuffling, clambering, crawling and climbing, we threaded our way into this strange forest. Everything was hushed, covered in a fine dust that stung the eyes, clogged the nose, and dried out the lips so that they cracked and itched. Then the fine dust worked its way through the cracks, drying out the inside of the mouth, so that the tongue swelled and made speech difficult. My ears ached, my hands felt caked. After hours of stumbling, choking and wheezing, half-blinded, I was thirsty such as I had never before been: this, I imagined, was what it must be like to die in a desert. All I could think of was water. And yet, dry as the place was, our torches did not set anything alight.

Then, it struck me that I had been staring at books for hours and not a single volume had any writing on its spine. They came in all shapes and sizes, mostly old and worn and faded, and they were all anonymous. No titles, no authors, no publishers.

At the top of a dune-like pile we stopped to rest. Idly, I picked up a book and, wondering about the contents, opened past the flyleaf. The first page was blank. So was the second. And the third, and the fourth. I opened the book to the middle. Blank. I flipped to a random page: this one was mostly blank, with a smear of dull grey along the bottom. The next page had a little more grey, not much. And so it went through the book: wherever I looked, it was either blank or contained a small grey smear. I picked up another volume from my feet: the same. And so was the next book.

I looked up at Vance. 'What is this place?'

Vance was biting his lower lip.

'I think,' he said, his voice cracked from the dust, 'that this is the Library store.' He looked around, at the book towers, the spires, the arches, the mounds, the mountains. All of books.

'Yes,' he continued, 'yes, it must be: this is the Place of Dead Books.'

I had never heard anything so pompous. I could even hear the capital letters in the way he spoke — the Place of Dead Books. Whenever I felt that the University could not get any more ridiculous, it surprised me. I started to laugh.

Laughing hurt. With every breath I gulped in mouthfuls of dust that coated my innards, turned my lungs to mud. But I had to laugh. Life, death, Moira, Alexa, Finch … even the mule. Rampaging librarians, insane clerks, lost academics. I laughed until overtaken by another fit of coughing.

Afterwards, Vance berated me.

'I understand that you're ignorant, so we shouldn't expect too much from you.' He had regained his confidence in the face of what he probably considered my impiety. 'So I'll try to explain it simply. It will be instructive for the students, too.'

He raised a finger for silence. 'A book contains ideas, arguments. Those ideas may be right or wrong, in the ascendant or refuted. They may be current or forgotten. Some are obscure, some are obtuse. But they are all still extant.'

Vance opened a book at random. The pages were blank.

'Sometimes, the life will go out of an idea. It will cease to be. The idea, the argument, has died. This is different to being wrong or refuted or ignored. Such ideas may battle on for centuries until they are rediscovered or rehabilitated. No, the death of an idea is altogether a deeper, more mysterious thing. It is not well understood: how does it happen? And why? Although we cannot answer these questions, we do know when it has happened. When the ideas in a book die, they drain out of it, drip by drip, clause by clause. And then one is left with this —' he dropped the book melodramatically back onto the pile '— an empty, withered book. And perhaps a congealed pool of ink on the ground below it.'

The silence was deep. We pondered the fate of so many ideas, once in the primes of their 'lives'. And then the silent death and a librarian finding the now-empty book. Then its delivery to this, its final resting place.

'Nonsense,' I said. One of the students hissed.

'Don't mock,' said Vance. 'This is a deep thing.'

I stood up. It was time to move on. Certainly, the sooner I got free of these lunatics and found myself in the company of the next batch of lunatics, the better.

'You're all mad,' I said. 'Everyone in this University.'

My time with Vance and the students was drawing to a close, although of course I didn't realise it then. I stormed off, slipping and sliding down the hillock of books, in what I thought was a halfway dignified manner. More likely I looked ridiculous.

After a few minutes, the rest of them followed. Were we going deeper into this place, or coming out the other side? Was there an 'other side'? Did the Place of Dead Books go on forever?

On we went, surrounded by a world of empty books, dust and dead ideas. And then, after forever, one of the students let out a shout. I looked around: she was pointing off to our right. There, in the distance, was an enormous double-spiral staircase. Of course!

I could have slapped myself. The Place of Dead Books was simply the bottom level in the multiple layers of discs that made up the levels of the Library. So this staircase would connect with the inner circles above and, ultimately, with the outermost circles, the

Reference Section and the relative sanity and safety of the University proper. However, there was still the question of all the levels above us crawling with murderous librarians. I remembered Moira and the blood and shook my head to clear the image.

Although the staircase was clearly not the way out, still we headed for it. Moths and flames: it was fascinating if only because it wasn't a pile of books.

As we closed on the staircase, I was surprised to see that it did not finish at this level, as I'd expected. Instead, the double spiral continued down, to at least another level. And I could feel something strange, almost forgotten, rising from the stairwell: damp. There was water down there. At last everyone stopped moving about and I could hear, from somewhere far away, water dripping.

We stood in a rough semicircle near the closest landing, staring down into the dark.

'Water,' I whispered. I had never been so thirsty in all my life.

Vance hissed. I looked up. The others were staring at me as though I had lost my mind.

'Those are the sewers,' he whispered.

'And? There'll be clean water somewhere,' and in fact it smelled like water deep underground, but not at all like a sewer. Of course it would be drinkable.

'Don't you know what's down there?' Vance shook my sleeve.

I waited for him to continue.

'That's the underlake,' he tugged at me.

I pulled away. 'There's water.'

'You can't go down there!'

I smiled. 'There's nothing to stop me. Or if there is, tell me what. Say what's down there.'

Vance fought with himself, trying to say the words. 'The undermonster! The undermonster is down there!'

Even in the dim light, I could see that Vance had gone pale. 'And that is your "thing"?' I spat.

A rage was building in me. Since the Isle of Goats I had been pushed, prodded and moved at the whim of others. A ghost who wouldn't leave me be, bloodstained librarians, arbitrary rules. Always being rushed from one place to the next, in search of barely-understood goals for questionable ends. I couldn't remember my last meal, or when I had slept. I wanted to be in charge again. No more!

Furious, I swung my fist in Vance's face. I was holding the butt of my pistol at the time, and the muzzle caught him on the cheek, tearing it open. Blood spattered across his face. I yelled, a strangled croak. Vance fell back and sideways; a couple of books slid away from under him, falling over the edge and landing a few steps down.

'Stop him,' Vance muttered, as I stepped past.

I turned back to face the students, and held the pistol horizontally, pointing at no one in particular and therefore at everyone in general. My earlier qualms about being a poor shot seemed to have evaporated.

There was a pause, a moment when things might have turned out differently. But the students did not rush me, they did not try to reason with me. Instead, they shrank away. And I stepped onto the staircase and began the long walk down to that water. I kept my eyes on them as I went, just in case they decided to make a dash for me after all. But they did not. Down the stairs I went, into darkness.

THE SANATORIUM

U^{p.}

    Up I rose, swimming or flying, out of the darkness I descended a short time, a lifetime, ago.

    I awoke briefly, surfacing on the shore of light. My right eye hurt as though gouged. I reached up to it, blinking, but my hands were bound. Somebody nearby muttered something about a lost eye and that was merely interesting until I realised they were talking about me. I drifted back into the dark water.

    And so I dangled off the edge of my life. Darkness and cold spread through me, seeping out from my right eye. I stared down the walls of wet grey rock, into nothing. Far away, down there somewhere, I knew, was Alexa. After a time, the darkness ebbed once more, and I pulled myself up that thin thread, back to the ledge from which I had fallen. I awoke.

    Before opening my eyes, I could tell that I lay in a lit room on a comfortable bed. There was a slight breeze. Wherever I was, it was quiet, except for someone coughing rather desultorily somewhere nearby.

I opened my eyes. Except that only one eye responded. I reached up to feel the other one: it was covered in cloth, a bandage, perhaps. It had not been a dream, my eye was injured.

Oh, I thought, please let it not be gone. Please let me have both eyes. Don't make me a cripple.

Gingerly, I reached up to the bandage. Just touching it sent arcs of pain through my skull, down my spine and out to my fingers and toes.

I gasped and sobbed, all at once.

'Oh,' someone said, 'E's awake!'

'Who?' someone else asked.

'The goner! Hello there!' The last words were lost in a fit of coughing.

I blinked a lop-sided blink, my remaining eye trying to focus. I was in a large, low-ceilinged room. The gloomy light of the University streamed from an open window somewhere to my left, supplemented by candles. It smelled of soap and linen and citrus and, faintly, vomit.

Slowly, trying not to jolt myself, I sat up and looked around.

On both sides were rows of beds, much like mine. The one to my immediate left was empty, but the one next to that contained an old man, sleeping. Next to him was the window. To my right was an empty bed. Then there was another fellow, sitting up and leaning on a pair of crutches, waving furiously to me and coughing. There were more beds to my right and also opposite me. All were empty. A young man and a fat middle-aged fellow sat at a table facing me, playing cards in their hands.

The card players nodded to me and then returned to their game.

'If he's up, then you'd better give him an orange,' the fat man said.

The cougher spluttered a minute, then caught his breath. 'Ah, yeah. Yeah, that's right, an orange! Just a mo ...'

He fumbled at a large bowl of oranges on a table near the foot of his bed. Then he hobbled around to me. He sat down, groaning and coughing softly.

'Ope you don't mind me takin' the liberty,' he said as he sat. 'It's a bit 'ard to stay on me pins.

'Ave an orange,' he said, gently placing a large fruit beside my head, 'and welcome to the Sanatorium. We thought you wasn't ever goin' to wake up. Good to see you've decided to stay on this side!' He smiled and then turned aside, coughing.

The fat man glanced up, smiled quickly and returned to his game. 'They like to make sure we have plenty of oranges. They say the oranges speed recovery.'

'Cups,' said the young man, playing a card. 'What happened to you?' he asked, not looking up.

The coughing man looked across at the card players. 'Now, Sharkey, don't be rude. The gentleman's only just woken! He'll tell us, in 'is own time.' He turned back to me.

'Don't mind Sharkey,' he said, conspiratorially, 'e doesn't mean to be rude, it's just 'is way, is all: a bit abrupt.'

I smiled to indicate I understood. Suddenly I felt sleepy again. I dozed off.

When I awoke, Sharkey and the fat man were still at their game. The coughing man was leaning over the table, watching. I also watched for a while, but could not follow the rules of the game. It was strangely peaceful, observing them as they played, completely engrossed. Sharkey — the young man — watched the fall of the cards and his own hand with gritted concentration. He rarely so much as blinked. When he spoke, it was to name a suit:

cups, or wands, or swords, or turtles. Occasionally he called 'arcane starfish', but that may have been the name of the game itself. The top of his head was completely bandaged.

Unlike Sharkey and the cougher, who wore normal day clothes, the fat man wore a bathrobe. He didn't appear to be visibly sick. He occasionally muttered a few words to the coughing man before returning to the game. He smiled a little more often than Sharkey, but was otherwise just as grim, particularly about the game. As play continued, neither he nor his younger opponent ever questioned a trick or made those small noises that players often make when marking small victories and setbacks. As far as I could tell, they were not gambling. There were no chits, no coins, no thing on the table that could be used as stakes. Nor did they call stakes, as occasionally happens in certain games. No, they simply played and played and played, doggedly.

The coughing man was older than the other two. His hair was long and stringy, and his smile showed that he lacked several teeth.

Feeling suddenly hungry, I reached around until I found the orange. Then, gingerly, I pulled myself up to a sitting position.

The three men at the table noticed me moving. The coughing man waved, then stopped to cough. He hobbled over.

'Ah!' he said, smiling his gap-tooth grin. 'Awake again. You're goin' from strength to strength!'

He sat down next to me as I chewed on my orange. Sour and sweet, the juice stung my lips. It was unbelievably delicious. How long had I been asleep?

He sat down, apologising for taking the liberty. 'We weren't properly introduced last time you were awake,' he said.

'I'm Coughin' Jack. That's as in —' he coughed gently '— and not as in the box you're buried in!'

Coughin' Jack laughed at his own joke. Predictably, the laughter was overwhelmed by a coughing fit.

He waved at the card players. 'And that's Sharkey and Mr Crimson.'

'Pleased to meet you,' said Mr Crimson. 'Wands,' said Sharkey.

'I'm pleased to meet you.' Was that my voice? It sounded far away and thin, like a dying breeze. How long had I been lying here?

Coughin' Jack leaned back a little, hands on the tops of his thighs. 'Well now,' he said, smiling, 'ain't this nice?'

'Arcane starfish,' said Sharkey.

'Where am I?' I asked. It suddenly seemed that, since coming to the University, I had been asking that question a lot.

'Ah,' said Sharkey, 'you're in the Sanatorium. You're lucky to be alive, fellah.'

'The Sanatorium?'

'Mmf,' said Mr Crimson. 'This is where injured and sick people — wands — come to recuperate. Sharkey here,' he nodded at his opponent, 'had a nasty fall from some scaffolding, so they gave him a good trepanning. Isn't that right, Sharkey dear?'

'Cups.'

'And I,' continued Mr Crimson, 'have been recovering from a fever. I expect to leave shortly. Unlike our friend Coughin' Jack, here. Isn't that right?'

Mr Crimson glanced at Coughin' Jack, and then went back to the game. Coughin' Jack looked down at the floor, his face drawn.

'Nah, it's true,' he said. 'I got the consumption, y'see. I'm not ever leavin' this place.' For a moment he looked across the

room, miserably. Then he glanced at me and the sad look
was dropped, replaced by a slow-spreading smile. 'But what's the
use in sadness, eh? As me old man used to say, self-pity's no use to
the livin'.'

'Aye,' said Mr Crimson.

'Butterflies,' said Sharkey.

'Double butterflies, return armadillo,' said Mr Crimson.

Assuming that my things were still with me, somewhere,
and that my money had not been stolen, I doubted that even then
would I have enough money to stay in a sanatorium. In my home
city, only the well-to-do could afford to stay in such places. Nor did
I have any relatives to bring me food. It occurred to me that I never
received that receipt for Just Mule and the rest of my things.

'I can't stay here,' I said. I wasn't sure if I could stand, let
alone walk. But I had to leave.

The card players paused, then continued their game.
Coughin' Jack looked worried.

'What do you mean?' he asked.

'A sanatorium,' I found it hard to breathe. 'The cost. I can't
afford it.'

'Ah,' said Coughin' Jack, who put a hand, reassuring and
restraining, on my shoulder. 'Not to worry. This place is free to
workers at the University. Part of the wages of the job, you might
say. You'll be cared for until you can move on. Relax, son.'

'Have an orange,' said Mr Crimson.

'Plugs,' said Sharkey.

I let that sink in. For the first time, the University seemed
more civilised than my home. There, sanatoria were places to
which the seriously ill and infectious members of well-to-do families
were sent to recover or die in isolation. One paid for the privilege of

a bed, and of course servants or family members brought food every day or paid for the sanatorium to provide it, at exorbitant rates. It was said that your family must hate you with a deep and abiding hatred to send you to a sanatorium. Then there were the sick-houses, places dirty, dank and diseased. A place where people went to die; the insane, the crippled and the beggar who collapses in the street. Such places were always sited next to crematoria.

I relaxed. 'How long have I been here?'

Coughin' Jack shrugged. 'More'n a week. What a mess you were, too!'

'That long?' No wonder I was so weak.

'Son, closer to two weeks. You were mostly dead when you got here. Missin' an eye and all cut up like that.'

I lay back, defeated. Across the ceiling was a faded fresco, pinks and blues. I couldn't make it out. So I really had lost an eye.

Coughin' Jack realised his mistake. 'Oh, mate, I'm sorry. What an eejut I am! Shouldn't ha' told you. Not my place. No, not my place.'

I shut my remaining eye. 'Are you sure?'

'Oh, I'm sorry. Yeah, sure as sure: the doctor who's been treatin' you told us some of it,' he said, sounding miserable.

'What happened?' I asked. So I was a cripple, after all. No longer a whole man.

'You were in a rowboat, down by the landin' where the charwomen do the laundry. They found you just before dawn. The boat was tied up, they say, pretty as you like, but with a strange kind of knot.

'The doctor — Lucrese is her name, you'll probably be seein' her this afternoon — said you were all beaten about. Your eye was gone, your face was covered in scratches. Just like a net was thrown over your face,' Lucrese said. 'And you was rantin' and ravin'. Wouldn't shut up. You kept going when they brought you here. Mostly nonsense. But my, you kept at it! You were telling someone something!'

'Pretty emphatic,' said Mr Crimson.

'Whoever you thought you were talkin' to, you certainly gave them a good telling off,' smiled Coughin' Jack.

'Lucrese told us,' said Mr Crimson, 'that you had an appointment to work at the Department of Information. Near as we can work out — wands — you must have been caught up in the last spate of unpleasantness at the Library.

'If so, you're a lucky man. I've heard eighteen people, not counting librarians, were killed.

'But what we can't work out is how you managed to travel from the Library to a boat moored to one of the laundry landings, and in your state. How did you get there?'

Mr Crimson's tone was a mix of concern and menace, like honey and wormwood. They turned to look at me. Even Sharkey stopped playing. I thought back. I remembered the Library, and the riot. I remembered escaping with the academic — what was his name? And going down the stairs. Down and down. To the Place of Dead Books. Or were the stairs after the Place of Dead Books? Before, or after, or both? I couldn't remember. And something about an underground coast. Something white that flashed and swam and fed. But my eye? How had I lost it? How did I come to be in a boat? Vague shapes turned and presented themselves to me, explanations or misinformation: but it was all so hazy and unreal. Like trying to see vapours hiding in a mist.

'I can't remember,' I said.

'There,' said Coughin' Jack, patting my shoulder, 'you've had a rotten shock. Rest. I'm sure it'll come back to you.'

'Pistachio reprise,' said Sharkey.

It did not come back to me. I lay on the bed, the taste of orange in my mouth and a lacework of faded paint and cracks on the ceiling, listening to the card players and their calls. After a while, Coughin' Jack got up and hobbled away, coughing softly to himself. He settled himself on his own bed, groaning slightly as he did so. Every so often a breeze touched my forehead and the tip of my nose. There was a dull ache in the place where my eye used to be. I wondered if it was healing cleanly. The backs of my hands itched. The quiet enveloped me. Far off, I thought I heard a crow.

In all the stories, the ones we use to frighten children, there is a monster at the bottom of the well. The monster devours children, but only the naughty ones. Be good, always be good. Do as your parents say. They are nearly gods and, one day, when they are dead, they will be gods and you will worship them at the family altar, just as they worship their parents and all the other ancestors. Always be good. The monster has flashing eyes and the most terrible sharp teeth. It swims at the bottom of the well, waiting for naughty children. The naughty children are thrown in by sad parents who have failed in their task of teaching their offspring the right way. If naughty children won't be taught, they must be devoured. The monster is white, like a pallid corpse. It swims and eats and eats and eats and eats and …

'Are you awake?'

I must have dozed off. I opened my eye. A woman was leaning over me, although at a professional distance. She was in her late thirties, perhaps, and wearing a spotless white robe.

I nodded. 'You're Lucrese?' I asked.

She smiled briefly. 'They talk too much here. Can you sit up?'

I nodded again and, delicately, raised myself.

'As you guessed, I'm Lucrese. I'm the doctor for this ward. We know who you are, Shipton, thanks to the papers that you had. You've had a nasty tangle with something, you know that?'

'I don't remember what happened.'

'I'm not surprised,' she said. 'Serious accident, after all. You might remember, perhaps you won't.'

She examined my eye, my tongue, my ears. She felt my throat and took my pulse. Her hands were warm and dry, her movements sure. At the same time, I noticed a subtle difference in the quality of the light coming from the window: a new day?

'Humours are good, pulse is normal. You had a fever, you know.' She stared into my eye, as though trying to read my past.

'What will happen now?' I asked.

Lucrese straightened. 'I'm sorry to tell you this, but the eye is gone. I'm afraid there's no way I can make it any easier.'

'I guessed,' I said.

The doctor gave me a compassionate look. 'I'm going to change that bandage now. After that?' She waved one hand. 'You'll get a solid meal. I want you to start exercising. Take a walk to the end of this room, look out the window and then come back to your bed. I'll see that hot, solid meals are brought to you. We've been pouring water and honey down your throat for more than a week, just to keep you alive.

'If the wound is continuing to heal as well as it has, then we should be able to remove the bandages for good in a day or so. Then you'll need a patch,' she paused, considering. 'Unless you want a glass eye.'

I looked down. I hadn't thought about what would happen when the eye — the wound that used to be an eye — was healed. A patch? A glass eye? Leave it so that the world could see my ruined face? I didn't like any of the options.

'Well,' she said, 'you've got plenty of time to consider. And they're not mutually exclusive, after all.'

Perhaps embarrassed, she came around behind me and began to unravel the bandage. She looked at the side of my face that I imagined must be a complete ruin. She didn't wince, however. Sharkey, Mr Crimson and Coughin' Jack were studiously playing or watching cards, making it clear that they were not looking at me, my face or anything at all to do with the consultation.

Lucrese made a clicking sound, smiled briefly again, and then re-bandaged my face. She threw the old bandage into a bucket.

'Nice. It's coming along nicely. Almost completely healed.'

'So what will happen next?'

She motioned to the bed, could she sit down? I nodded.

'Well, because your papers were found in the boat, it was clear that you had been hired by the University. The Department of Information has been informed about you; I understand that you were to have taken up a position with them. There was some confusion because you didn't arrive and they assumed that you had decided not to work there. They've taken on someone else for that position; however, they asked that you be sent on to them anyway.

'Once you've got the strength, you can leave. It shouldn't be more than a few weeks.'

After Lucrese left, Coughin' Jack hobbled back to my bed, brandishing an orange.

'Here,' he said, placing it by my hand, 'eat this now. Food'll be here in a bit, and then you should do what the doctor tells you. Have a walk, yeah?'

The food, when it came, brought on trays by a pair of grinning porters, was good. It consisted of a soup that was halfway to being porridge, hot, with chunks of meat and vegetables. But not strongly flavoured, although spiced with cloves and white pepper. There was weak beer and coarse bread, and of course an orange apiece.

Neither Sharkey nor Mr Crimson moved when the food came in, although Coughin' Jack fairly yelped with pleasure and hobbled over to the servitors as they came in, waving each arm in turn while supporting himself on the crutch under his other arm and smelling the bowls and smacking his chops like an old dog. When the food was brought over to the card players, they placed their cards face-down on the table and, without comment or even looking at each other, began to eat. Both players used exactly the same technique to eat: first, they spooned around the bowl until they found a chunk of meat or vegetable, then they lifted that to their mouths. Blow on it to cool it, and then into the mouth. A few rapid chews, and then a swallow that looked painful. And then onto the next chunk. Were there an exactly equal number of chunks in each bowl? And if so, who was employed to count them? Having finished the solid portion of the soup, the two men, as though by prearrangement, but I guessed more likely beccause of long habit, lifted their bowls to their lips and, slowly and with delight, drank the porridge-soup. Then the bread, tearing off a hunk and chewing rapidly. Then the beer, drained almost at a draught. Then the orange.

Finally, they sat back and, facing each other, spoke.

'A good meal,' sighed Mr Crimson, patting his stomach.

Sharkey belched. He picked his teeth with a fingernail, and then shrugged, as if to say, 'It was passable.'

Mr Crimson shook his head. 'D'y'know, Sharkey dear, that you have perhaps the worst table manners in the world?'

Sharkey grinned. 'Nyah. You should have met my father.'

'Bad, was he?'

'Terrible!' Sharkey's grin grew even wider, and he stretched, arms wide. Then he brought them together and cracked his knuckles. 'He was a roof repairer in the south wing maintenance division for twenty years before he retired. The old man never learned to use a fork, always called them "focks" and thought they were sissy. A real man uses his fingers and a knife, he'd tell us.

'And he didn't believe in napkins, either. My mam couldn't never get him to use one. Still, he was a good roof repairer.'

There was a pause. I realised that the conversation, like the way they ate, was a ritual, something they did at every meal.

Mr Crimson stood up, pressed his hands to the small of his back, and stretched. There was a loud crack.

'Oof,' he said. 'A good game. Yes, a very good game indeed.'

He sat down, and gestured to the cards. 'Well, and shall we continue?'

Sharkey grunted and they picked up their hands. Play resumed.

I'd been so interested in this interchange that I'd forgotten to eat my own food. I set to, suddenly realising how hungry I was.

After eating, I lay back on the bed. It felt good to have a stomach full of warm food. There was nothing to worry about, nowhere I needed to be. The colours and cracks on the ceiling formed and re-formed into vague, half-sensible images. Never quite one thing or the other, they tantalised, half reminding me of things and places. Things. My things. Lucrese had mentioned my papers, and the others had hinted that my belongings were here around about. I was wearing my own clothes, although they had been washed and put back on me at some time while I was unconscious.

With a start, I sat up. My things!

I looked around and there, on the floor near the bed, were my purse and saddlebags. I picked up the purse. Empty.

'My money,' I murmured, not realising I had spoken aloud. I felt the saddlebags: the pistols and their case were all there, at least.

The card players stopped. Coughin' Jack coughed, more to get my attention than for relief.

'Ah,' he said. 'Yes. That'll be the washerfolk who found you. Thievin' sods, the lot.'

He looked down, as did the card players. Sharkey muttered, 'Seven of wombats.'

Coughin' Jack coughed again, then smiled inanely. 'You'll be wantin' to take that walk!'

Oh well. Foolish to think that my money, little as I had left, would still be there. A purse of coins would be too much temptation for even the most honest of persons, especially if it looked as though the rightful owner might die.

Little by little, I eased out of the bed. Standing on the floor in my bare feet, I couldn't quite work up the energy to take a step. It was all I could do to remain upright. I began to slide. Then there was a strong arm under mine, and a shoulder to lean on.

'We'd best make this fairly quick,' Sharkey said, beside me. 'I'm losing valuable card time here.'

Step by weak, ponderous, shuffling step, Sharkey and I made our way to the window. It ran from floor to ceiling, and I realised it was a door that opened out onto a balcony. Through the white curtains I could see a balustrade and some chairs.

We passed the old man. When the food had been brought in earlier, no one had bothered to wake the sleeper, not even to drip water and honey down his throat. The old man's face was flushed, and a strange odour came off him. It was sweet and heavy, and reminded me of something in a well.

At last we reached the balcony. Stepping through, I turned to Sharkey.

'Thanks, I want to stay here awhile.'

He eased me into a chair. 'If that's what you want. Call out when you're ready and I'll help you back to bed.'

I sat on the chair, gazing up into the grey sky. Around me, buildings spun up like fingers of grey stone. Far off, black dots sailed in the sky. I could hear crows. The air smelled clean, of the sea and rain. My legs and buttocks felt drained of all energy, my arms heavy. It wasn't cold at all.

'Almost pleasant, all things considered,' said Finch, close to my ear.

I was not surprised to hear him. As I had gone out to the balcony, I had half-realised that I was seeking solitude in order to see the spectre again.

'Finch. Always a pleasure.'

Finch laughed, a dry chuckle.

'I'd like to say the same, but you're looking a little the worse for wear.' Finch chuckled again, and the laughter held no warmth. 'Indeed, I'd say that perhaps now we don't resemble each other as once we did.'

I didn't bother turning to look at him. 'Remind me why I'm here.'

'Why,' he said, 'you and I made a deal. Don't you remember?'

'No. Or I do, and I'm testing you.' I was suddenly very bored with Finch and his games.

There was a pause. Then a hiss that I imagine was Finch sucking his breath in between his teeth. That didn't make sense: why would a ghost make a noise like that? Surely he didn't breathe?

'Shipton, you would do well to consider that I am the master and you are my creature,' hissed Finch.

I tried to laugh, hoping I sounded nonchalant.

'Really?' I said. 'I don't think so. I'm a free man.'

'How can you be free? Do you remember how you lost your eye?'

Damn Finch.

I didn't like to admit it, but he had a point. If I did not know how I had come to be where I am, how could I possibly know where I was going? The point was clear. Still ... something smacked of casuistry.

'I thought not.' Finch made a noise that might have been spitting. 'Between you and me, you're only here because I want you to be. You'd have been dead a thousand times over if I had not saved you. Again and again I've had to intervene, over and over again, just so that you could keep your head above water. Even a child can do that — but you, you're useless. Why did I ever choose you?'

Head above water. Why did that phrase strike me?

Finch continued. 'On the Isle of Goats, you could have died, had I not intervened. How foolish, to take one's own life! Look at everything you would have missed. The scrumptious Moira, for instance. And that woman, married to the no-hoper carriage driver. What was her name? Ah yes. Mary. Nice dish, too. You could have either of them, you know. Or even both. Or even both at once. You'd like that.'

'Finch, you're sickening.' But it was true. I realised that I wanted them, wanted them both. Even if I had seen Moira bloodied and baying for more blood. Even if it meant breaking Mary's and Polk's hearts.

'Sex, money, power. I can supply these, if you do what I want, creature. It's not much. Just do my bidding.'

I was finding it hard to argue with the spectre, or even remember why I might want to argue.

'But why?' I wanted to ask, but why am I still alive?

Finch misunderstood. 'Because I'll be very grateful. That's why. I can give you as much money and power and sex as you want. They are none of them any use to a dead man. No. All I want is vengeance. And you're going to give it to me, oh yes. And I'll be very grateful, you'll see. We have a deal. Always did. Remember, Shipton, I understand you. No one else does.'

Finally, I could ask the question. 'But why aren't I drowned? I was found in a boat.'

It didn't make sense. Somewhere, there was a gap in his words, a way I could see through to the lie I knew must be lurking there. Something happened to me before I was found, something that showed Finch up for what he was.

'I am not entirely without means,' replied Finch. My arm was suddenly very cold, and ached as though bruised. I looked down, and saw Finch's hand resting on my shoulder. He was looking at me, and I looked at him. My master. Suddenly I was afraid: how could I feel him touch me like that? Was he becoming more real, or was I becoming less?

———————

The days passed, and life settled into a routine. We were fed twice a day, mid-morning and early evening. The food was always filling, hot and nutritious; however, the constant intake of oranges did become tiresome. Eventually I stopped eating them altogether, until Coughin' Jack got agitated by this, and I took to having one every day, just to quieten him. The card game continued. Never once did I see either Mr Crimson or Sharkey, who always took a break to help me walk to the balcony and back, exchange more than a handful of words not strictly related to the game. They always seemed to be playing when I awoke in the morning, and played after I had gone to sleep in the evenings. Even when I was restless and woke in the small hours, they would be there with a lamp, playing away. I suppose they slept, but I never saw it.

We were expected to bathe every second day. For this, one of the porters would help me down the hall to the bathing room. On the way, we passed a number of rooms like mine. The porter told me that there were another four rooms for women, on another floor. Male and female patients were kept separate, as were children and the insane. Almost all doctors were women, and the Sanatorium was considered one of the best places to work, because the food was good — it had its own kitchen, whereas the rest of the University used the communal kitchens, of which the less said the better — and because duties were light. Helping the sick to recover meant doing very little oneself, apparently.

I became particularly friendly with Parr, a porter who had been employed at the Sanatorium for at least forty years. Unlike many of the porters and other workers in the University, who inherited their position from their father or mother, depending on the job and tradition, Parr had, like me, managed to get a job by external application. As he understood it, the University needed to hire about a tenth of its entire population of general workers every year: for some reason, the internal population did not replace its numbers and was forever in decline. So fresh blood was needed. And there were few people interested in entering the University as a worker; mostly they wanted to be students or scholars. So the difficulties put up in front of people who came looking for jobs were really tests of tenacity, since few were turned away. Bribing the officials helped, but wasn't necessary.

Eventually, Parr told me that there was another sick room on this level. It was always locked, and food and clean linen were sent in, and dirty linen retrieved, by a dumbwaiter arrangement. Nobody went in, except to die; and nobody came out, except as corpses. The Isolation Room, as it was known, contained only one kind of case, those with a disease called the cryp. According to Parr, the cryp was always fatal. Nobody knew how it was spread, nor were there any effective treatments: hence the isolation. It was a reasonably rare disease, but every year there were ten or so cases. Rumour had it that the cryp was the result of a curse laid on the University, that when built, workmen had been sealed up in its walls by accident, and the cryp was their vengeance.

'Somethin' about vengeance that has its own logic, y'know?' And he spat.

Parr, however, considered himself a man of science, as befitted a porter with a position at the Sanatorium, and so he did not hold with such tales, exciting as they might be when told over a mug of ale by a fire. No, he believed what Lucrese and the other doctors had told him, that the cryp was merely an exhalation of the brackish swamp on which the University had been built. A recrudescence of timeworn corruption, although that wasn't the phrase Parr used.

He explained that I was lucky to be alive, not just because of my injuries, but because the washerfolk had debated killing me for my coin and my pistols. In the end, it was the nature of the scratches on my face and chest, now healed to a patchwork of fine lines, and the strange knot used to secure the dinghy, that decided the issue in my favour. Scared of the things that dwell in the underparts of the University, they had decided to leave me alone and report the find. They hadn't so much as touched me.

Parr told me other things. The old man in my room was dying, and that was why he wasn't disturbed. He was the last of his line, and he was being given the dignity of death without interruption. The meat in the soup was mule. Apparently there was no shortage of unclaimed mules in the stables. As fruits for aiding recovery, lemons were more efficacious than oranges, but no one could be induced to eat them. And the card players were indeed playing Arcane Starfish, games of which sometimes lasted generations.

Sharkey and Mr Crimson were rough diamonds. Sharkey would never work on the repair scaffolding again, although that was his life and his livelihood, his family's traditional work. Since a job with the University was a job for life, he would be relocated to an office somewhere, or he'd be trained as a porter. A young man, energetic and supple and strong, he had no wish to stay behind a desk. His intense interest in the card game was merely a way of avoiding having to think about what the future held for him. It would come soon enough.

Otherwise, Sharkey was a gentle soul. He was always ready to help me, in the early days when I could not properly support my own weight. Once or twice, he left the game to plump up the old man's pillow.

As for Mr Crimson, his title was due him as a tutor of undergraduates. His area of expertise was the Mathematics of

Impossible Numbers. I tried to appear interested when he explained this to me, but he was obviously used to other people's disinterest and incomprehension, and did not try to tell me more than that it was based on the twin ideas of the square root of negative one, and that positive one was not in fact a prime number, because it was evenly divisible by one and another number, which was as yet unrevealed to the discipline. Economists were very interested in the theoretical work carried out by impossible mathematicians. They didn't understand it; they were merely interested in it, and their incomprehension did not stop them using it as the foundation for their own work.

Mr Crimson's department was quite close to the Department of Information, and he invited me to come visit him some time. By now, Coughin' Jack and Parr had both explained to me that Mr Crimson, like Coughin' Jack, would never leave the Sanatorium. He had a canker that daily was spreading itself through him. He was here to stay, here to die. Of the five of us in this room, only Sharkey and I would leave the Sanatorium still breathing, and only I had any prospects.

Lucrese. Lucrese came by every second day to examine each of us in turn. She always began with Coughin' Jack, then Mr Crimson, Sharkey, the old man and, finally, me. After two weeks, I realised that I was anticipating her visits with a kind of delicious suspense. I enjoyed watching her examine the others while pretending not to watch. Did I ever catch her eye, ever so accidentally, during these moments? I looked forward to her touch on my forehead, a few kind words that signified nothing at all, but in my imagination I could weave into hidden messages, elaborate codes.

In these weeks I was not once disturbed by Finch.

And so I was ready to leave. I had decided to wear an eyepatch, rather than a glass eye. It seemed more honest. My face, shoulders and chest were a craze of lines, mostly parallel. I looked strange.

Two days before I was due to leave, I told Lucrese that I wanted to see the place where I had been found.

'I hope that it will help me remember something.' Since coming to the Sanatorium, everything that had happened before, even those parts that I remembered quite well, seemed events in someone else's life. I had been thinking it over and I thought there was a good chance that revisiting the site might help me to remember.

Lucrese looked at me without blinking. 'I think that's a good idea. I'll take you there tomorrow.'

The next day, Lucrese and I went from the Sanatorium out onto an overcast, grassy field. Then into another building, down stairs. And stairs. Across corridors, near halls where lecturers were expounding or students were shouting them down. We were overtaken by running students or crept around dozing porters. Eventually, we came to a long corridor from the far end of which heat, steam, light and a dull roar emanated. The humidity and heat increased with almost every step, until my undershirt was soaked with perspiration. At the end of the corridor, we came out into a cavern where almost the entire floor was covered with barrels filled with steaming water. All around the barrels, people stirred the water with long sticks or bashed cloth against the edges. There were huge fires burning at either end, the heat from which kept the entire room tropically hot, while also heating enormous vats of water. Through the air, pipes soared and knotted and branched, leading from the vats to numberless spigots, one for each barrel. Around the barrels rushed burly, red-faced men and women. The air was so humid I could barely breathe.

'The laundry,' Lucrese murmured. 'These are all washerfolk.'

On we went, past the washing room, to an arched corridor. As we reached the end, the corridor opened out onto a landing. At intervals, stone steps led down to short wooden piers. The water was only two or three metres below us. Above, impossibly high, yawned the walls of the University. And stretching out in front lapped the waters of the bay, the bluffs ahead the only break in blue-grey water, blue sky. Blue sky! I had forgotten what that looked like. Out there, where the gulls wheeled, were sky and clouds not poisoned by the University's presence. The University was its own cryp, poisoning itself.

Along the walls, to our left and right, great mechanisms of wood and rope held enormous loads of laundry, flapping and drying in the sea breeze and reflected sunshine.

Lucrese pointed to one of the piers. 'Down there was where they found you, that one.'

I took a few steps forward, then turned to Lucrese. She and I went down the steps, onto the pier.

I stared at my feet. Nothing. What had happened to me? I lost an eye — why couldn't I remember? I shook my head. 'No.'

I looked up. Lucrese regarded me with her unblinking look. 'Nothing?'

'Something,' I said. She was very close.

She didn't blink, didn't flinch. So I kissed her. She looked surprised, and then she shut her eyes and responded. I kept my eyes open: I was terrified that if I shut them, when I opened them again, she would be Finch. Or Alexa. Or a white thing that lives in the deepest bottom of a well and is cold and hungry.

She stayed Lucrese.

The kiss ended, abruptly, when she broke contact. She was breathing a little heavily. So was I.

'I know nobody like you,' she said.

I touched her cheek. That broke the spell.

She turned away, took a half step back so that we couldn't kiss again.

'It's not allowed for a doctor to touch a patient like that. Never.' She turned completely away.

'I won't be a patient in a day.'

She looked back, half-smiling. 'That's true.' Her smile faded. 'But I swore an oath, and I won't split hairs.'

We walked back in silence. Only once did she speak.

'Tell me the truth: did you ask me to take you to there,' she waved behind her, to indicate the place of the washerfolk, 'just to get me alone?'

'No,' I murmured.

And to be honest, I had no idea why I'd touched her. Yes, I was attracted to her, although she was more than ten years my senior. Was she married? Did she prefer girls? I knew nothing about her. Was I even interested in her? Did I perhaps get carried away by the moment, the closeness of a woman's body? My own need?

I felt sordid and disappointed and ashamed.

THE DEPARTMENT

I left the Sanatorium the next day. Lucrese pronounced me fit to leave and take up my duties in the University. Her examination, as always, was deft and thorough: no word or sign suggested that anything had passed between us the previous day. She did not say goodbye.

I was sad to be leaving. The Sanatorium had been a welcome respite from the winds of the bizarre and grotesque that blew through the rest of the University. I knew I could not stay: I was not coming any closer to finding a way to rid myself of Finch, and so had to move on.

My departure was brief. Sharkey and Mr Crimson ceased their game long enough to stand and shake my hand. Coughin' Jack gave me a last orange, making me promise to come and visit them. I said I would, and at the time I meant it.

So I found myself walking across a quadrangle with Parr, who had been assigned to act as my guide to the Department of Information. In my saddlebags I carried my hat, my empty purse, the pistols in their case and a load of missing memories. I still had the Aardvark's papers for Professor Margolis tucked in my coat. I felt strangely light, as though a burden I hadn't known I carried had fallen away somewhere back in the Sanatorium.

Once again I plunged into the maze of the University. Interiors, gloomy and sullen, succeeded dull and grey overcast quadrangles. We crossed bridges, passed beneath balconies, walked along corridors and echoed, skipping, through empty rooms of dust and stale memories.

Soon — or after an eternity — we came to a long, low and wide hall, lined with shelves on both sides. These were interspersed with doors to the right and windows to the left. The shelves were mostly empty, with only an old mop or rag here and there. At the very end were double doors of some dark wood, with frosted glass set along the top half. Above the doors were painted a pair of eyes, so fashioned as to follow one around the hall. We approached the doors, and I saw the wood was inscribed with the legend, 'Division of Information' and below this, 'We know what you do not'. My heart sank.

'Well,' said Parr. 'Here 'tis.'

We glanced at each other.

'Now,' he continued, 'you'll be fine. Do you have your papers?'

I nodded, feeling strangely like a small boy being left alone for the first time.

He patted me on the shoulder, then shook my hand.

'It's been an honour and a pleasure,' he said.

I smiled with what I hoped was a brave-looking smile. 'For me too.'

'Well,' he said, and brought his hands to his sides. After a moment, he turned and walked away, down the corridor. I watched him go, then listened to his footsteps until they faded in the gloom.

I took a deep breath, turned and faced the door. It occurred to me that I could turn and run. There was nothing to make me go through that door. But I sensed that Finch was very close to me, and would never let me get away. What choice did I have? I opened the door.

On the other side was a long corridor, wider to the left of the door than the right. There were a few aging palms in pots at intervals along the wall near the windows on the left. To my right were a series of closed doors, each leading presumably to an office or set of rooms. On my immediate right was a counter, behind which sat a severe-looking woman.

I stood, gazing stupidly at her as she wrote in a large ledger. After a minute or two, she looked up.

'Help you?' she asked in a nasal voice. The tone suggested it was very unlikely, in her opinion, that she could help, or that she would if she could. In fact, she'd rather enjoy being of no help to me at all.

'I have a position here,' I said.

Her eyebrows shot up so far and fast I thought they might achieve flight. 'Oh?' was all she said.

I told her my name.

Reluctantly, her eyebrows worked their way back down her forehead.

'Ah. I remember: Shipton. You were unwell. And just when the rush was on, too. Most inconvenient.'

There didn't seem much I could say to that. I kept my peace.

After a while, she continued. 'Well, Professor Margolis is not in at present. You can wait over there.' She pointed opposite, to a blank stretch of wall.

'Thank you,' I said. She returned to her ledger and I, dismissed, slunk over to the wall. I put down my things and leaned against it.

I watched the departmental secretary — for I assumed that was what she was — writing in her ledger. Occasionally, she got up and walked around her little office, taking out and opening files kept in drawers along the back wall. On one occasion, she ate a biscuit.

My mind wandered, and I thought about Lucrese and then, with a pang, Alexa. Somehow, I knew that Finch had seen the kiss, and he would not let it go unremarked. I would pay for that. I could imagine what he'd spout when next he chose to reveal himself to me. Did he reveal himself, in fact? Or did he come and go? When I couldn't see him, was that because, as spectres are rumoured to do, he had made himself invisible? Or was it because he had simply left, gone on to who-knows-what ghostly backroom? I imagined that Finch was a kind of spectral actor, and his departures were to a dressing room well beyond the curtain that separated this world from his. There he would touch up the greasepaint and rehearse his lines.

I started to laugh at the thought, and then tried to suppress it, so the noise I made was a snort, something like a pig snuffling up a stone. It was about as painful, too. The secretary glanced up, looking at me as though I'd gone mad.

I turned away. From this angle I could see through one of the windows. It looked out from several storeys above onto a wide, grassed area, fringed with sickly-looking plane trees. Among the trees were stalls, and moving here and there in great waves and eddies and swirls were people: students and scholars, workers and hawkers. I was staring at one of the great boulevardes, similar to the one which led to the entrance of the Library, except this one was open to the sky. I had gathered from talking to the others at the Sanatorium that the boulevardes were all connected, so in fact, if I went down to the boulevarde and walked in one direction or the other, I would eventually either find the Library or run out of boulevardes. If that happened, then the Library was in the other direction.

I felt a strange elation, a recurrence of that lightness when I left the Sanatorium. A weight had gone, one I hadn't realised I carried. Although I was looking out on an area of the University that I had never seen before, I felt less bewildered than usual: I had recognised a connection, made sense of some part of the geography. However small it was, a map was beginning to form in my head. I was basically lost, but not as lost as before.

The doors behind me were opened, and something swooshed past. At the same time, the departmental secretary yelled, 'Professor, professor!'

I turned at the same time as the person walking past stopped, and so came face to face with a smallish woman, about a head shorter than I. She was wearing a scarlet dress instead of the cowled habits almost all students and scholars wore, with a scarlet fur collar. On her sharp nose perched a pair of dark half-rimmed glasses, over which she peered with a mercilessness I'd only ever seen in the eyes of my uncle's hawk.

'Professor Margolis,' said the departmental secretary.

'Yes, Wendy,' the woman replied, not taking her eyes off mine.

'This is the new assistant. Name of Shipton,' Wendy said.

Professor Margolis smiled a slow, thin smile. She held out a hand. I took it, but she did not grasp mine or shake. Instead, she removed it, let it slide out from mine.

'I understand,' she said, 'that you can do things.'

I'd forgotten how impressed the Aardvark had been with that. Oh, well.

'Yes, I can do things.'

'What kind of things?' She didn't blink.

'Um,' I said, it being the first thing that came to mind. I hadn't expected to be asked what things I could do. Margolis was less insane than the Aardvark, it seemed. And a damn sight smarter. I suddenly felt that I was trapped with a hawk.

'"Um"? You can do "um"? That'll get you far around here.' Her smile dropped and she turned around, stalking off.

I realised that my position with the department was not so secure as I'd been led to believe. I had to wrest something out of this situation, which was spiralling out of my control.

'Any things,' I called after her. 'What things need doing?' I wasn't entirely unaware of the sexual undertone of what I'd just said.

Margolis glanced at me over her shoulder and stopped walking. She smiled. 'You'll do,' she said.

I followed her down the corridor and into her office.

The room was large, with full-length windows opposite the door. Another door led off to the left. Bookshelves, crammed with books and papers and manuscripts and wax rolls and recording devices I didn't recognise, ran all around all four walls, filling every available space, except for one spot where a samovar bubbled. In the centre of the room was a large desk, with a large leather chair. Near the desk was a set of filing cabinets, atop which was a globe. Beyond the desk was a rug and a leather couch. A few wooden chairs, mostly supporting books and papers, were scattered about the room.

Margolis threw herself onto the couch, and lay there with one arm over her eyes. She waved vaguely towards the desk.

'Sit there,' she said.

I moved to the high-backed chair and, placing my things under the desk, sat down. The surface of the desk was polished. There was a leather blotter and a few papers and books piled at the margins. A few pens stood in a stand. There was a frame for a picture, but it was empty, as was a small vase that stood next to it.

Margolis sighed, an exhausted sound.

'Shouldn't be so tired,' she mumbled. 'Only mid-morning.'

I stared down at my hands.

'Well,' she said, glancing at me before putting her arm over her face again. 'It was a good day for my discipline, the area of study under which the Department of Information "lives", so to speak. Well, do you know what happened today?'

I shook my head, realised she couldn't see me, and said, 'No.'

'Ah. Today our discipline was accorded something like its true importance. We've been moved two circles deeper into the Library! The collections of my discipline — Meaning — and the Military Sciences are to be swapped, starting this afternoon. In exchanging places, we will also be promoted above Law. Those seige engineers are going to get a taste of their own medicine! Let's see how they like being dropped out. Good news.'

I wondered if this would cause another riot. Perhaps not: from what Parr and the others at the Sanatorium had told me, reorganisations did not always cause the librarians to go on the rampage.

She waved one hand airily. 'Make me tea,' she commanded, pointing to the samovar.

Since my duties had yet to be made explicit, I supposed they included making her tea, at least temporarily. I knew about tea, of course; however, I had never made it with a samovar before. I hoped it was simply a matter of pouring it out into a cup. The device had a spigot, cups and a bowl of sugar cubes. I turned the spigot, and a brownish liquid came out: unmistakably tea, and strong. I placed two cubes on the saucer and, rattling the cup slightly as I walked, took it over to her.

She pointed at a slightly brown spot on the rug. 'There.'

I put the cup where indicated, and withdrew to my station at the desk.

After a few minutes, she half pulled herself up, reached around for the cup and saucer and, without taking her eyes off me, sat it on one of the wide armrests. She glanced at it. 'Two sugars, good. Don't make mistakes around me and you'll get on just fine.'

She dropped one cube into the tiny teacup, where it dissolved into the tea, turning it into a kind of thin sludge. Then she placed the second cup between her teeth and, watching me closely, drained the cup at a go. It was very hot, but she didn't seem to notice. She sighed and put the cup on the ground.

'Why were you sick? I had to put up with a buffoon in your stead. You're not a buffoon, are you?' She fired the questions off like a platoon of soldiers.

'No buffoon, no.'

'Hmm.' She sniffed. 'Well, we'll see. And the sickness? What happened?'

I spread my hands. 'I'm afraid I don't remember.'

'No? A pity.' She sighed again, as though preparing for an unpleasant duty.

'Right,' she said. 'let me explain how this works. I am a Professor of Information Theory with interests in Informatics, Informology, Informography and Applied Stuff. In normal rotation, I head this department once every three years, a privilege and a duty I share with professors Wax and McMuffy. I have a number of students assigned for postgraduate work, as well as teaching several undergraduate courses.

'You, on the other hand, are some semi-literate from beyond the University who the Aardvark has managed to dredge up. You may be of some use to me, but probably you'll have to learn everything I need you to know, rather than being instinctively aware of it. The very fact that I have to tell you your duties, as I am about to do, is evidence of how backward and uneducated you really are.'

I cut in: 'So you have no time for people who need to learn things that you already know?'

'That's correct,' she said, without a trace of irony. 'Nor should I have to put up with people such as you not knowing things when I need you to know them. Sadly, I have to bear with your limitations, it seems.'

Margolis made a steeple with her fingers. Her look was both disapproving and predatory.

'Now,' she said, 'for the most part, you will take dictation for me. My thoughts are free, unfettered, original and very important. I cannot be expected to both have the thoughts and write them down. No, that's just not acceptable. It will be your task to write my thoughts as I have them. I will lie on the couch and tell you what to write. Is that simple enough for you?'

I nodded.

'Good. Pleased. Now, I cannot be expected to break my concentration in order to explain concepts to you. And certainly, I will not stop to spell unfamiliar words or the names of my colleagues, on the rare occasions when I'll make reference to them.

'I expect you to know all this beforehand, or to familiarise yourself with it in your own time. If you don't understand a concept or a word or how to spell someone's name, then look them up.' She waved a hand, vaguely indicating the four walls packed with books and papers and whatnot.

'Again, that'll be in your own time.

'Further, it is not acceptable that I should slow the force of ideas for your benefit. I expect you to write very fast. Indeed, I expect you to write faster than that. If you can't keep up, then learn to do so. Make whatever effort is necessary, my words are not to be lost.'

I opened my mouth to ask what my hours were. She raised her voice, ever so sligthly.

'Never interrupt me. You speak only when I give you leave. Otherwise it'll be chaos. These are my rooms, and there is only room here for my voice.' She raised an eyebrow, as though daring me to challenge her. Not likely. 'I don't care if you've broken a leg, you don't whimper unless I explicitly give you permission.'

She lay back down. 'When I don't specifically need you, I expect you to be out of sight.' Margolis pointed to one of the side doors. 'There's an office in there. Use it to do the boring tasks. Apart from dictation, you'll answer my unimportant correspondence — which is most of it — and I expect you to not make any mistakes there, either. There may also be some routine paperwork: I have no idea, it's your job to find out about that from Wendy. Get whatever she needs from this office for her, and don't bother me with it. Did you have a question?'

'Yes.' I almost stuttered. 'What exactly are my hours?'

Margolis shrugged. 'You're to be available whenever I need you to take dictation. That could be at any hour. I suggest you sleep under the desk in your office.'

This sounded like an impossible arrangement. I suspected worse was coming.

'Do you have any other questions?'

'Professor Margolis, I was told that, while I was sick, you replaced me. The buffoon? What happened to him?'

Margolis didn't blink. 'You assume a male.'

'Well, what happened to her, then?'

'It was a male. He was inappropriate, unacceptable. He fell off a balcony. Gone to the Sanatorium.'

I wondered whether, about the time my replacement was ready to leave the Sanatorium, I might not be found to be unacceptable or inappropriate and find myself falling off a balcony. I had no doubt that she would do it.

She placed her hand on her face, theatrically. 'Do you have any more questions? After this, I will not accept any further questions.'

I might have asked her where the writing-paper was kept, but I didn't want to waste my last question on something so prosaic. Instead, I had found my attention being drawn more and more to a globe that stood at about chest height on the filing cabinet. At first, I dismissed it with a cursory glance. Then, as my eyes wandered around the room during Professor Margolis' various tirades, I noticed that the globe was entirely sealed in a clear glass sphere, and that what appeared to be a miniature, snub telescope was mounted on a brass armature that was attached to the stand of the globe. It wasn't possible to turn the globe, but it was possible to adjust the telescope's bracket or armature so that it could point to any portion of the globe. The telescope pointed towards the globe, so that viewing the globe through the telescope would bring part of the world into huge relief. It reminded me of nothing so much as a strangely-proportioned microscope.

As I returned, again and again, to the globe, I realised that the clouds that I at first thought were painted on were actually some distance off its surface. They were floating around the globe. And then I realised that the globe was neither supported by a column nor suspended by a wire: it hung, completely against all sense and gravity, in the dead centre of the glass sphere.

So, in answer to her question, I pointed at the sphere and asked, 'What is that?'

She glanced up from behind her hand, looking at me, my hand and then where it pointed.

'That? Oh, that,' she said unconcernedly. But it was clear the lack of concern was feigned and that she was secretly pleased. Proud of the object? Or perhaps she had feared a prosaic question, such as the location of the writing-paper. Perhaps both.

She sat up and, using that tone of voice people have when they are very interested and knowledgeable and enthusiastic about a topic, but fear the listener is none of these, answered: 'That is the Best of All Possible Worlds.'

I must have looked as blank as I felt.

She sighed with the enormity of it all. 'The Best of All Possible Worlds. It's a philosophical tool.'

'How?' I'd asked another question, but I suspect she forgave that one.

'The Best of All Possible Worlds is an intellectual device sometimes used by philosophers. The test goes like this: can we imagine that something, or that a state of affairs, might exist? If a philosopher wants to know whether a particular state of affairs might pertain, they could formulate it as, "In the Best of All

Possible Worlds, such-and-such a thing might be true." It's a test of reasonableness. After all, before we know if something is the case, it might help to imagine whether such a state could be possible, on other worlds if not this one. And of course that leads us to conditions on the best of all possible worlds.'

She stopped. I must have looked as confused as I felt.

Margolis sighed again. 'Well, it's not significant exactly what the Best of All Possible Worlds is, only that there is a best world among all the worlds that might exist, and that's it there.' She waved at the globe.

'So that world is better than our own?' I asked.

She nodded. 'And every other possible world, every alternative. Better than them all.'

'It must be a paradise,' I said, wistfully.

'Hardly.' Margolis snorted. 'Frankly, it's better than our world, I'll grant you that. But only by a little. The wars are bloody, but not quite so bloody as ours. The poverty and hunger are slightly less than here. The ignorance is there, but more that of a near-grown porker than the full-blooded pig-ignorance we have. Lives are short and miserable, but a little longer and a little less miserable than our own. The hatreds are slightly less intense, the rapes are slightly less common, the taxes are infinitesimally less severe, the corruption just a smidgen off our own. They laugh a little more, but not much; the flowers are a bit brighter, but fade just as rapidly. Honey is sweeter, salt saltier: but only a little. Screws fall out, wheels fall off, holes grow in buckets.

'When all is said and done, the Best of All Possible Worlds is not that much better than our own. In fact it's a borderline shitheap.'

Professor Margolis lay down again, covering her face with a scarlet handkerchief.

'All of which leads me to only one conclusion,' she said, waving one hand in the air. 'Tea.'

'Tea?'

'Get me tea,' she growled. I bolted from my chair, recovered her cup and brought her a fresh one. After she had drunk it, she continued.

'The conclusion I reach is that if the Best of All Possible Worlds is only marginally better than our own, and the world we inhabit is such a mess, then it can only be because the Creator is an incompetent. Or possibly a cretin. The bastard.'

My jaw dropped. I had never heard such blasphemy!

She sat bolt upright. 'But who cares what the Best of All Possible Worlds is like or what it tells us? The important thing is that all the philosophers want it, and I've got it!'

She smiled, a mean and hungry smile. 'And they'll never get it. Almost as good as getting the Philosopher's Stone from the Alchemy Department. Not that I've got it. Yet.' The last word was spoken in an undertone.

'Now it's time to take dictation!'

I almost fell off my chair.

Well, I did the best that I could. Professor Margolis spoke rapidly from beneath her scarlet handkerchief, ideas and phrases and concepts flying from her lips. I had not the training to make even minimal sense of what she said: there were so many words that I had never heard before, and much was in other languages that

I didn't speak. I wasn't even sure where we shaded from my own tongue to the others when she spoke, except that every so often she would return to our language and, with a jolt, I would realise that I hadn't been writing down what she'd been saying, or that I'd been trying to copy it phonetically. She never once looked up at me, simply rambling in her strident way, leaping around concepts like a gibbon in the jungle. I doubted that she remembered a tenth of anything she said, and wondered how many of her secretaries had taken down even that much.

My attention began to wander. At first, I wondered how old she was. At least fifty, I thought. I wondered how she came to be here, in this room, spouting nonsense — or what sounded to me like nonsense, and after coming to the University I'd become quite a connoiseur of it. And why was there a portrait frame on her desk, with no portrait in it? Whose picture had it once held? A lover, a husband? A family?

However, what really interested me was the Best of All Possible Worlds. Could it have been true, what she told me? An entire world, just like ours, only better? And that the best possible wasn't particularly good? On reflection, I realised that part made sense: the best world of all only had to be better than the rest, slightly less mediocre. But what if, on an absolute scale, slightly less mediocre was still near perfection? Or at least near perfection in the eyes of the One who Made All? I pondered what she had said about the Creator, and wondered if it could be true, that part about incompetence. A potter who could not mould clay. I remembered my ancestors and felt impious.

Surely Margolis had been making it up? There couldn't seriously be people like us, but infinitesimally small, living on that little globe? I resolved to find out.

After several hours, Margolis petered out. Thinking that she might remember the last thing she'd spoken, I hurriedly wrote it down. The thinker on the couch was silent. Nothing moved. I guessed she was asleep.

Quietly, so as not to disturb her, I stood up from the desk and, picking up my things, tiptoed to the door where she'd indicated my office was to be. The door was not locked. I stuck my head around the corner and saw a room not altogether much larger than a broom cupboard. It was mostly filled by a battered-looking desk. There were old-fashioned quills, some ledgers, a rickety chair, a dusty cushion and some candle stubs. A jug of what was probably wine and a dry brown loaf completed the scene of cheer. I dumped my things on the desk and, quietly, returned to my place.

—————

For four days, my duties were thus: Whenever she had nothing better to do, Professor Margolis dictated to me. It was impossible to keep up with her or understand her. After the second day, even my feeble attempts to take down some of what she said became impossible because my wrist seized up. The pain was astonishing, but I kept my mouth shut. She could talk for hours, at any time of the day or night. I would be woken from my naps curled up in my cupboard, and given one minute's notice to be ready. My door could not be locked, so I was available at all times. Her rooms were through the other door, and whenever she entertained other academics or students, always male, I was expected to keep to my room and keep my mouth and ears shut. Many of her gentlemen visitors were invited into her private chambers. Sooner or later (usually sooner), they would be ejected, looking ashamed and small. Then I would be summoned to take dictation. Before she began, she would invariably complain.

'There aren't any true men left, not like …' and then she would sigh, glance at the empty picture frame on the desk, put her hands on her hips, and dictate. After a while, she'd flop on the settee. Not once did she ever ask me to read back to her or show her what I'd taken down. At first I tried to file her thoughts, but the filing cabinets were empty, legacy of a long line of disgruntled buffoons. So much for a system I could follow.

She had to give lectures every day, which meant there were times where I could be definitely free of her. It was during those two-hour stretches that I explored the area around the department. I learned how to reach the boulevarde, and in which direction the Library was. I briefly considered visiting Moira, but decided it was too far to go in two hours, and almost convinced myself that that was the real reason I didn't go.

As I explored, I began to form a better picture of my surrounds. I felt less at the whim of others, more able to look after myself. I had felt powerless for so long in this place that even a mild understanding of the space around me boosted my morale. Although I was a virtual prisoner to Margolis' overpowering personality, I became more confident that, if I needed to, I could get away. Lack of money was still a problem, however.

It was during Margolis' absences that Wendy brought me bread and wine. She was a good deal less abrupt than she'd at first been. She explained that, as far as the department was concerned, my wages were met in full by being provided with food, drink and 'adequate' accommodation. That said, if I survived Margolis for a year, one of the other professors would probably poach me, and that almost certainly entailed a pay rise. In the meantime, there were certain funds she could release if I was in need. As far as I could gather, there were a number of assistants like myself, working in similar conditions, although none of their masters were quite as sadistic as Professor Margolis. When I asked Wendy about the additional duties, such as the correspondence, of which I could find no evidence, she just laughed. There was no such thing, although Margolis and the rest imagined that they received adoring letters from the outside and that their writings were read and known, anticipated, throughout the world. They had enormously false impressions as to their own importance.

'If you tell them that virtually no one outside the department has ever heard of them, let alone outside the University, they'd be so incredulous, they'd forget to get angry at you,' was how Wendy put it.

Of course, I spent as much time as I could staring down the telescope at the Best of All Possible Worlds. I couldn't see a thing. No matter how I toyed with the instruments, all I saw was a fuzzy white patch with some wisps of blue-green along one edge. If there were indeed people down there, they were hidden. Margolis was mad.

On the other hand, it seemed that almost everybody was mad here, so why her madness in particular should bother me, I couldn't say. Perhaps because there was so much spite in it, and she seemed to have power enough to act on it. She was not a person to be crossed. I was worried that, sooner or later, she'd invite me into her private chambers. I had no idea what would happen then, but given the fate of her other guests, I suspected I'd end up falling from the balcony.

After my third week, Professor Margolis entrusted me to take a message to the Aardvark. She was lying on the couch, dictating. Today she wore a purple dress. Throwing the matching purple handkerchief from her eyes, she sat upright, switching topics in mid-sentence.

'This is intolerable!' she barked. My pen shot into the air, spraying ink across the page. 'Damn it! I can't spare you! No, not for an instant! I won't!'

I picked up the pen, and, knowing better than to ask questions, waited for her to continue.

'That bastard!' she yelled. 'How dare he? Who does he think he is?'

She stood up and walked over to me, dropping a letter onto the desk. It was sealed in wax with McMuffy's seal, McMuffy being the current head of department.

'He thinks he can do whatever he likes, just because he's the head! Wait 'til it's my turn, then I'll get him!'

After a while, she calmed down enough to notice me. 'You're to deliver that letter to the Aardvark. We need to hire some more assistants for some project McMuffy has cooked up. He thinks he's worked out a way to snare syllogisms.

'Well, I've got to give a special seminar series this afternoon and tonight, so he thinks you're not needed here. Pah! I tried to tell him about the correspondence you're seeing to, but he expects you to do that some other time. He's just envious because he doesn't get as much.'

I stared at the blotter, trying hard not to smile.

And that was how, two hours later, I found myself walking to the Aardvark's office with coin in my purse (for incidentals, according to Wendy) and a half-formed plan never to return. I knew where I was going, and Finch could go to hell. If he wasn't already there.

Between the map Wendy gave me, and asking directions from students and porters, I was able to reach the Aardvark's office within an hour and a half. I took no wrong turns, did not lose my way and, thankfully, was not accosted by Finch. I was surprised by that: I had become accustomed to his company, although I didn't welcome it, whenever I was alone for long periods. But I had not been troubled by him since we talked at the Sanatorium that one time. So happy, I whistled. I knew where I was going after the Aardvark.

The office was as I remembered it.

'Yes? Yes? Come in! Yes?' huffed the Aardvark, moments after I stepped into the office.

Peter sat at his desk, watching me from under his brows, while pretending to write something on the papers in front of him. The Aardvark stood on his desk, hands clasped behind his back, rocking from toes to heels and back.

'Come in? Hmm. Oh, you're in. Well,' he clapped his hands, then stuck them around back again, 'No matter.'

He snapped his fingers and Peter rushed around from his desk carrying a folding stool. He placed it directly in front of me. The Aardvark climbed off his own desk, came around, and climbed the stool. From there he looked down on me slightly.

'Do I know you?'

I shrugged. 'You gave me a position here. Don't you remember?'

'Don't remember. Don't trust one-eyed men. Nope. Never trust them. Hmm.' He squinted at me with one eye and then the other.

'I had both eyes then.'

Peter clapped in delight, and the Aardvark raised a finger.

'Aha! That would explain it,' he said. 'What's your business here now?'

I handed the letter over to him. 'This is from the head of the Department of Information.'

The Aardvark stared at it, and then sniffed it, as though it were a dead animal. He waved at it, and Peter came over to take it from me. Peter turned it over in his hands, looking at the seal.

'It's the departmental seal, all right,' he said.

I held up my hand. 'I was instructed that no one but the Aardvark was to open it.' Nobody had given me any such instruction, but I couldn't help it.

Peter looked disappointed. He handed the envelope up to the Aardvark, who opened it and, without looking at it, passed it straight back to Peter, who immediately brightened. I had to hand it to the Aardvark, he knew the tricks.

The clerk read the letter in silence, then said, 'We're instructed to hire an additional two research assistants for a new project.'

The Aardvark rolled his eyes, then stared at the ceiling. 'What do they do with them up there? Eat them?' Then he remembered I was there, and muttered, 'I meant that only metaphorically. No need to repeat, is there? Good, good.'

I took a step backward and bowed, in the ancient manner. For just a moment, my eyes left his, and I glanced at the ground near my feet. It was not until I again stood upright that my sluggish brain registered what I saw and, stiffening, I looked down again.

The Aardvark, solicitous now because of his error of judgement in slighting the department when an employee was present, spoke at twice his normal speed, going so far as to touch my shoulder.

'My good man, nothing wrong is there? Something we can help you with?'

I was looking at the Aardvark's desk. At some point since my last visit, the table leg had somehow become shorter again and he or, more likely, Peter, had propped it up with more personnel files. These were not covered in dust, and from the covers saw they were requests for places for students. The name on the topmost file was Polk.

Polk, waiting out there in the village of Drab, riding his cart, getting older and slower and more disillusioned. A wife and children, the wife growing more and more lined, fatter and more shrewish. Happiness giving way to deep bitterness and emptiness, always living in the shadow of his dreams, never achieving them. Never climbing the walls and storming the citadel. And now it was within my power to change that. Was there something they could help me with? Of course there was.

'No,' I said. 'Nothing.'

I knew where I was going.

NOCTURNE

It struck me as odd, as I walked away from the Aardvark's office, that Polk's fate had not been sealed long ago. Instead, it had come down to me. Some never get onto the first rungs of the ladder of life: they go a little way, far enough to see the ladder before them, but for whatever reason, fate or lack of courage, they do not even take the first step up. Polk was one of these. When I saw his file holding up the Aardvark's desk, I knew that, with a word, I could resurrect his hopes. I had the power to help him and did not. I enjoyed that: the pleasure of the bully.

As I crossed the quadrangle that led to the Sanatorium, it occurred to me that, under Margolis' unintending tuition, I was daily growing more mean and spiteful than Finch. Perhaps that was what I needed to defeat him.

Through the wrought iron gates that mark the boundary of the Sanatorium grounds. Across the sickly lawn, fringed by thyme and fennel, to the stone steps. Into the hall, seen only once before. Across the marble floor, to the spiral staircase. Up the staircase to the first floor, the offices of the doctors. Along the corridor I read the names on the doors, until I came to Lucrese's. I knocked on the door.

At first, there was no answer, and I feared she was not in. Perhaps on her rounds?

Then a muffled, 'Yes?'

The door opened. There she stood in a white cowled robe, the hood down at the back and her hair free. Her eyes widened.

I said nothing. I did not blink.

She looked down and sideways, then back to me. Then she stepped aside.

It was late in the afternoon and the room was lit by an old-fashioned oil lamp that gave everything a soft yellow sheen. A desk and a single bunk, a chest for clothes. A vase containing flowers I didn't recognise, some books. The eternal bowl of oranges.

She shook her head. 'Shouldn't have let you in,' she said and then closed the door.

I couldn't take my eyes off her.

She looked back at me. Both of us panting. Something had changed between us, altering the subtle play of power. Then I realised.

'I'm not your patient any more.' I did not smile.

Again, she shook her head. 'Even so. You were, once.'

'Changes. There are changes.' Neither of us moved. She, back to the door, and me, awkward between the pallet and the table.

'Would you like an orange?' She smiled.

I laughed, looking down at the bowl of oranges.

'It seems to me,' she said, 'that you are followed by demons. They are everywhere, all around you. You're here to slay demons, aren't you?'

I nodded. 'And you are here to heal.'

There's the sound of clothes sliding away from skin.

'You're right,' she said. 'You're not my patient anymore.'

Afterwards, Lucrese and I lay together, head in shoulder hollow, close on the tiny pallet. Breaths and heartbeats, body fluids and warmth. I wondered who I was, why I was there. Secure, close to dozing.

She touched my cheeks with her fingertips. In the gloom, I could tell she was facing me because I felt her breath on my cheek.

'Awake?' she asked. I said yes.

'Are you sure you wouldn't like an orange?' She laughed and gently punched my chest.

'Are these your quarters?' I asked.

'Yes, but it's possible to get larger ones. If I think I'm going to be entertaining regularly.'

'I'd like that,' I replied.

'But …' she said, pre-empting me, aware that I was about to reject her offer and, by extension, reject her.

'But … but, but, but. There's always a but. What you said about slaying demons, it's true. It may be that being too near me would not be wise.' I stroked her lips, so that she couldn't answer.

It was getting late and I needed to return to the department before I was missed. I sat up and collected my clothes from where they dropped. I dressed, and Lucrese formed a half-circle around me with her body. She touched my leg.

'You're not returning, are you?' Her voice was thick, silently crying, not wanting to let me know. But the time after intimacy is when secrets are hardest to keep.

Will I return? I couldn't say. I would like to. But I wondered if I would live long enough: I suspect that Finch's mission of revenge does not include an avenue in which I keep my head attached to my shoulders.

'Yes,' I said, and it might not even be a lie.

I left, then. I've left my seed within her, and my smell on her sheets, her pillow. These will fade, and then I'll be only a memory. And eventually, I won't even be that.

Out her door I passed, along the corridor, down the steps, across the marble entrance, out the wrought-iron gates, past the sleeping porter. Parr? I can't tell in the starlight. And then I left the Sanatorium and plunged once again into the world of the University.

———————

As I walked, my mind turned to Alexa. I felt no pang, either of loss or of shame. Indeed, for the first time since her death, I was able to consider my wife with equanimity. Elfin, mischievous, light-coloured, young, she was in many ways the counter to dark, older, grave Lucrese. I had grieved for her and held vigil, but I felt now that I had earned some life and intimacy. In all likelihood, I would die soon, so it mattered little. I thought of men killed shortly after ejaculation: their seed might outlive them, the only living part of a dead body. And if that seed found purchase, produced new life, after the death of the man?

I don't know why I felt doomed. The feeling had started during our lovemaking. There had been an abyss, glimpsed but briefly and then hurriedly denied. My real reason for leaving her so quickly was because the mantle of demon slayer rested too easily on my shoulders. What she had called me seemed too natural. Demon slayers don't live very long, as all the legends tell us, and those near them are liable to be hurt or killed. Otherwise, I might have stayed in Lucrese's bed forever, and the hell with Finch or Margolis.

In the legends, the demon slayer always goes into the underworld and makes a pact with the powers that dwell there. In return for a gift of blood, or a loved one, or a limb or member — say, an eye — the demon slayer returns with the knowledge needed to kill the demons that plague the world.

Is that what happened to me? Is that how I lost my eye?

As I walked, I realised that Finch was near. How I knew that, I could not say. But I knew it. And I knew that he was excited.

And there he was, leaning against a grubby plane tree in an otherwise deserted quadrangle. He touched his fingers to the brim of his hat.

'Pleasant night for it. Or perhaps not?' he said. It occurred to me that he'd used almost those exact words on the Isle of Goats.

'Finch,' I said, as neutrally as I could.

He moved his head slightly, and starlight fell across his face. His eyes were glowing, a dangerous and cold fire.

'Well,' he said, chuckling coldly, 'I must say how impressed and surprised I am.'

'What is it?' I wanted him to get on with it, and so quickly finish his usual round of taunts.

'Here I am, thinking you were lusting after that librarian or that slice from the village! And then this doctor! My, my: you're quite a fellow.'

I glared, feeling uselessly angry. I started to walk away, and then thought of that night on the gallows hill. I was not strong enough to walk away from Finch.

He continued, oblivious. 'And doesn't she make some entertaining little noises, hmm?'

I spat at his feet: a challenge to a duel. Instantly, he punched a finger into my cheek, just under my good eye. I flinched, but did not turn away: his finger felt like a frozen knife blade.

He hissed. 'You are my creature and you will treat me with the respect due.'

'Creature I may be,' I said, rubbing one hand against my chest, 'and yet you are a demon.'

I wondered if he understood the significance of that comment. I suppose he did, because he began to laugh, a long and low wheezing chuckle. He stopped laughing, and punched me in the face. My legs fell away beneath me, and I landed on my bum. The cheek under my good eye stung as though it had been torn open and then lemon juice poured in. Tears filled my eye, and I rubbed the cheek. Already it was hardening into a swollen bruise.

'Watch yourself,' he spat. He looked at his own fist, seemingly surprised. Then he calmed a little, and took a step back.

'We've passed through much together,' he said, in a conciliatory tone. 'You must know that I want only this small thing, and then you shall see how grateful I can be.'

As I stood up, I felt — strangely, perversely — that goading Finch to the point where he raised a hand to me in violence was a victory. I had made him so angry that he had struck out, rather than using clever words and ruses. It proved, too, what I had suspected since I saw him at the Sanatorium, that he was becoming more solid; at least, he was becoming more solid in relation to me. No will-o'-the-wisp, although a spectre he might be. If he could touch me, then I could touch him. And that meant that it was possible I could harm him. I doubted that something so mundane as a flintlock ball would be effective. As werewolves are said to require silver, so too Finch wouldn't be despatched in a commonplace way.

Finch was talking. He spread his hands, palms down, and then turned them over. 'It's soon. I want you to stay alert, always keep your pistols loaded and on your person.'

'What are you talking about, Finch?'

He looked at me as though I were a dunce. 'Why, revenge. Revenge, creature. The time is coming, it's going to be very soon, now.'

Something like excitement shot through me. 'You mean?'

Finch smiled. His eyes were so cold, so brittle! 'I mean that. Do not forget our arrangement. I promised you much and, in return, you promised to carry out a small service for me. And soon, you'll do it.'

I waited. 'Go on.'

'There is a man that you have agreed to kill for me. You are close, very close. Soon you will meet him, and I want you to be prepared for that. You might not get another chance. He must, I want him to, die.' Finch made a fist, brought it down into his open palm. 'Die.'

'You've never told me why you want him dead.' I shook my head, wondering. And why could Finch not do it himself, if he could hit me?

'Why I want him to die is of no concern to you, creature,' Finch muttered. 'Although, suffice it to say, as I have done in the past for your benefit, that he hurt me, took away everything I had. It was he who drove me to suicide on that island.

'More than that, you don't need to know. You agreed, and disclosure was not part of the bargain.'

'It's not enough, Finch. I need to know.'

Finch's look was an uneasy mix of compassion and distaste.

'My poor creature,' he began, 'you know you can't do without me. You tried walking away from me once before, and failed. Remember?'

Again, the gallows. I nodded, looking at my feet.

'And I'm the only one who understands you. I know what you feel. And I've given you a purpose. Aren't you grateful?'

I thought I was angry, thought I was going to disobey. But why should I? Perhaps Finch was my master, not a demon to be slain.

'You'll be ready?' He asked, intent.

I shrugged, opened my hands. 'I'll be ready.'

Finch smiled, long and slow and hungry. 'Good. See that you are. Remember to take the chance with both hands when it comes.'

I glanced at a shadow moving across the quadrangle, a cat. Then back at Finch, but he was gone. I turned and continued to retrace my steps, back to the department.

So the time had almost come. It thrilled and appalled me: for so long now I had lived with this ghost at my shoulder, always taunting and tempting me. He had shown me what really dwelled deep in the recesses, or the absence, that I was pleased to call myself. And I hadn't liked it at all, had learned to dislike myself as thoroughly and as venomously as I disliked that spectre. He was a bastard, and I was just like him; or had become so.

The reason for all this was his drive for vengeance. And I was to be the instrument of that, the weapon that killed on his behalf. But I was not just a weapon, I was a human being. No matter how much Finch might want it — or even I might want it, if it meant freedom from the ghost — I was not certain that I could simply kill another person. Even if they were a perfect stranger to me, as I suspected Finch's target would be.

Could it really be happening?

Strangely elated, eager and appalled, I returned to the department. Margolis had not yet returned. I lit the lamps and, somehow knowing that this time my attempt to see would be different, placed one by the Best of All Possible Worlds and sat at the telescope. I peered down into the eyepiece and, adjusting the focus ring, saw the clouds, and then saw a gap in them. I could have laughed out loud: there is a way of seeing the hidden, if only one is lucky enough to stumble on it.

Through the telescope, I saw a deep, dark forest. On all sides of this forest, war raged. It was a ferocious war, and the towns and villages, fields and dams were all devastated. The forest remained untouched, save for damage at its outskirts. Armies marched, their faces covered by masks, their hands covered by gauntlets. They did not know why they fought, they only knew that they had always fought this war, that the enemy were most certainly in the wrong, and that their cause was just, their opponents' cause nefarious.

Deep in the forest, there grew an enormous tree. It was the great-great-grandfather and -mother of all the trees in the forest, and perhaps all the trees in the world. Its base was wider than a cathedral, and it stood high above the rest of the forest, providing shelter and protection, its outspread branches proof against any lightning strike. Beneath their sheltering ancestor, the trees of the forest grew and spread their seeds.

In the branches of this tree was one particular branch. Ancient and gnarled, it had died centuries before, but due to the play of chance and fate, had not broken away from the main stem. It was on this branch that a village had been founded, formed of people who had escaped the war and now sought peace, high up in the branches of the grandfather tree.

Life was not easy on the dead branch. For a start, there were no safety barriers, so the least false step, while running or walking tipsy late at night, say, could have irrevocable consequences. Also, the branch waved somewhat in strong winds, so that those who did not have a good sense of balance and a better sense of reaction might fall. Finally, because the branch was dead, it could at any moment give way. Thus, it was imperative that nobody make any sudden movements or take up dancing that involved jumping a lot, such as jigs. The villagers lived in constant fear of a loud cracking noise and a sudden lurch, the moment when everything would be dropped into oblivion.

So why did the villagers live in such a difficult place? Mainly, they lived there because they had always lived there. The oldest, who had founded the village when the war first began, couldn't remember the time before they had arrived, and certainly were beyond remembering by what deductions and deliberations the group had decided to settle on a dead branch high up in the most ancient of trees.

Certain thinkers had, in the past, suggested moving to one of the living branches. Such suggestions had been met with much stroking of beards and dark mutterings. After all, the village had always stood where it stood and, despite the admitted dangers and uncertainties, it was home. No one knew what the other branches were like: much safer to stay put.

Such was what I saw when I looked at the world that is better than ours, but only by a little. When Professor Margolis returned, she had me take dictation for six hours.

A JOURNEY
OF REVENGE

Finch was right when he said his revenge would be soon, but perhaps he hadn't realised how soon. It was the next day. Early that morning I was already awake and waiting in my accustomed place at the desk for Professor Margolis. She came out from her chambers dressed completely in peacock blue.

'There you are,' she said, as though she'd been searching for me. 'Why aren't you ready?'

She assumed, as usual, that I knew something simply because she did.

I stood up, trying to determine what was expected of me without asking.

'Hurry up!' she snapped. 'Can't keep Professor Finch waiting all day.'

A thread of ice worked its way through me, starting with my bowels and ending somewhere in my chest, all the while retaining a grip on my throat. I forgot the rule about asking questions. 'Did you say Finch?'

She looked at me with disgust.

'How dare you!' she said, throwing an empty teacup at me. 'I'll have you dismissed for that!'

She looked around for another teacup.

'Professor Finch … he'll be waiting,' I ventured. That distracted her.

'Oh,' she said, putting the back of her hand on her forehead, 'damn it. We can't keep the professor waiting.' Then she remembered me. 'Well? Why aren't you ready?'

I wasn't sure what would constitute 'being ready', but I ducked into my broom cupboard and put on my coat and tricorn hat. I saw the saddlebags, containing my pistols. The spectre, the other Finch, had told me to be ready at all times. To kill. I saw the bags, I saw myself open them. I saw the pistols, heavy and blunt, in my hands. I watched the hands as they placed them on the table and carefully loaded them. And I watched as my hands placed them in my inside coat pockets. They bulged stupidly, and the coat was pulled slightly down, just enough to make the coat shoulders rub, but the pistols weren't going to fall out.

Professor Margolis looked mollified when I returned. As I passed the desk, I picked up a sheaf of blank papers and a pen-and-inkstone set. We left her rooms, me slightly behind, went down the hall and out of the Department of Information. Downstairs, across the wide boulevarde, which I now knew as the Boulevarde of Heroes, and into one of the more ferocious-looking towers: Philosophy. The foyer was wide, studded with what I at first thought were stalagmites, but then saw were busts, most of them roughly hewn. As we passed one, I glanced at the plaque. It was the name of an ancient philosopher, a head of the department. The busts were strewn about the entry in no apparent order, or perhaps in a kind of order that could only be glimpsed from a different perspective.

'Professor Finch and I are to debate today. It's an important issue, do not miss a word,' Margolis said over her shoulder as we began to climb the stairs in the centre of the foyer.

Corridors branched to left and right, front and back, sometimes above and below. Margolis continued up the staircase as it narrowed and spiralled, higher and higher. And there I was, a pace or two behind her.

'We are to debate, in public, on "Mind Over Matter". I will take the part of matter, naturally,' she said.

Naturally, I thought, not understanding in the slightest.

Finch, Finch, Finch: the name was too big a coincidence. Was he a relative? Could it be that he was the man I was to kill? Yes, he was. I did not know how I knew that, but it was true: he was the one.

With every step, I was closing on my victim.

A man I'd never met, probably. A man with whom I had no quarrel. Could I kill him? Did I have it within me, murder? And what was his relationship with the spectre? Was the professor a father, brother, uncle or — horrors — son?

None of these. I remembered something. Elusive, hard to know where the memory came from, but related in some way to the time when I lost my eye, and undeniably true: 'Finch' was not the spectre's real name. Where had I heard that? And why did I believe it? The spectre had taken the name of his opponent, purely for my benefit. So that I would recognise who I was to kill without the need for the spectre's presence.

'Hurry up,' Margolis said, although I had not lagged behind. 'We must pay our respects to Professor Finch in his own chambers, before we go to the hall for the debate proper.'

Higher up we went.

'Although you obviously don't know it,' here she clicked her tongue, as though my ignorance would be the death of her, 'these inter-departmental and inter-disciplinary debates are very important for promoting collegiality across the University. And it will give me an opportunity to see if they really have got themselves a Philosopher's Stone.'

I wasn't paying attention. I was thinking about the man I was going to meet. Was he light or dark, tall or short, fat or thin? Who was he? What did he like to eat? Was he married, a bachelor or a widow? Was he brave or cowardly? Was he liked or loved or at least respected?

And with every step, I closed on my quarry.

I saw myself as a missile, loosed from its bow, winging to its target. Or a hawk, released and now stooping towards its prey.

I saw myself as I really was: none of these, merely a man, and a weak one, led on to a fate that I neither comprehended nor welcomed, the creature or servant of a ghost, whose schemes I could not penetrate. I was a cog in another's machine. No slayer of demons, me.

We were in one of the towers that surmounted the philosophy building. After a few more circuits, we came to a door, inscribed with the words: 'Professor Josef Finch'. We had arrived, and my heart was in my mouth.

Margolis knocked on the door. Then, when there was no immediate response, she knocked again, this time a little louder.

'Yes?' we heard, from the other side of the door.

'Professor Finch, it is I, Professor Margolis. I've come to pay my respects before the debate.'

'Ah, well,' came the response. Then the sound of bolts being drawn. 'Welcome.'

The door opened, and there stood Professor Josef Finch.

There are moments when it seems that time stands still. Time does not stand still, of course — it never does — but for a few moments, one is able to perceive everything. Nothing is hidden and it is possible to act far more quickly than others nearby and one becomes, temporarily, unstoppable. That's how it was for me at that moment.

Professor Finch stood in the doorway in a felt suit, a fez on his head. He had a goatee and was a short man, not quite as tall as Margolis. He did not look unkind. He was in his sixties or seventies, perhaps a little stooped with age. He opened his mouth to say something.

Whatever he was going to say, he didn't get a chance because I moved. Before I thought, knowing that thinking would undo me, I acted. I stepped forward, pushing him in the chest. The air rushed from his lungs as, taken by surprise and off-balance, he fell backwards. I stepped into the room, swinging on one heel.

Don't pretend that there is something dishonourable in a man striking a woman. In an emergency, it's permissible to do whatever is required to stay alive. If that means throwing babies to sharks or children to crocodiles, then so be it. I pushed Margolis back, just as hard as I could. She had time to grunt as my push forced the air from her lungs, and then she fell back down about three steps. I slammed the door and shot the top and bottom bolts while behind me there was a crashing sound as Finch hit the floor.

I turned as time returned to normal. The old man had hit an occasional table when he fell, overturning it. Painfully, he rose to his hands and knees, at the same time trying to catch his breath. Through the door I could hear Margolis screaming and yelling, the sound fading as she took off down the stairs, seeking help. I didn't have long.

I kicked the old man in the stomach, so hard he lifted off the ground for an instant. He started to cough, trying not to choke on his spittle. His hands and legs gave way under him. He wheezed and panted.

I can't say I didn't enjoy kicking the old man. It was a pleasure akin to the one I felt in withholding Polk's application. The pleasure of being mean and spiteful when one could be otherwise. That fierce joy of harming the defenceless.

He kept wheezing, trying to catch his breath.

'Finch?' I yelled. 'Are you here, Finch?'

He nodded, perplexed.

'Not you,' I hissed. For the fun of it, I trod on his hand. He gasped and something cracked. His hand shook and he took it, tenderly, in the other one. Holding it to his chest, he rolled into a ball, still trying to breathe.

'That's enough,' said Finch-the-ghost.

He stood beside me, arms crossed, staring down at the old man. Then the spectre crossed to the fireplace, hands out to the warmth. My Finch could never stay away from heat. 'You've done well.'

I shouldn't have cared what spectral Finch thought, but like a puppy, I found my tail wagging for the small bone of praise that he tossed to me.

'Please, please,' whined the old man. He'd regained his breath. 'What do you want? I have money. Gold.'

'It was easier than I thought,' I said.

'Who are you talking to?' asked the old man.

My Finch, my master, crossed the room. He stood directly in front of the old professor, and bent forward, peering into the man's upturned face. Clearly, Professor Finch couldn't see the ghost.

'Ah, Finch,' said the spectre. 'I've waited a long time for this. You laughed then. Laughed loud. My job, my ideas, my woman, my life. Well. Laugh no more. It was all mine by rights, you know. Not that bitter hard island, the rope. They should have been yours.'

Perhaps, for only a moment, the ghost revealed himself to the old man. The latter's eyes changed focus, gazing at and into the hot glittering hungriness of the ghost's eyes. The old man's eyes widened in shock, then recognition and, finally, fear. He gasped.

The spectre stood up and walked back to the fire. It laughed. 'Ah, creature. Alexa would be proud, if she could see you now.'

Alexa. The spectre overstepped the mark when he mentioned her. She wouldn't have been proud of me, and would have thrown it in my face if I had done something as mean as this in her honour. How could I hurt an old man for her sake? She would rather have died than that I do such a thing.

I shook my head.

'I won't kill him,' I said.

The old man opened his eyes wide.

'Don't give me that,' said the ghost. 'You'll kill him. And you'll probably enjoy it, although not as much as me. You're a kind of imperfect version of myself, do you know that?'

I stared at the pistol in my hand. How had that got there?

'No,' I said.

'Yes,' said Finch.

'Please,' said the living Finch.

'I won't kill him, Finch,' I said.

'Yes you will!' burst the ghost. 'I haven't come this far to have my revenge thwarted by you and your uninteresting little moral quirks! You'll do as I say!'

I shook my head. 'He's old, Finch.'

And it was true. I repeated: 'He's just an old man. No harm to anyone. And I won't kill him.'

The old man whispered, loud enough for us both to hear, 'But his name's not Finch. I'm Finch.'

We both looked at the man lying there as though he were irrelevant.

'That old man, whatever he did to you, it was long ago. Killing him now can't change things, can't restore you to life. I won't kill an old man for your benefit, Finch.' The pistol was so heavy. 'He's old.'

'But,' whispered the old man again.

'I don't care! I don't care if he's an old man! I knew he would be! You might be surprised by that, but I'm not! I waited decades on that island for you to come along. I was waiting for you before you were even born! Me! I!' Finch the ghost punched himself in the chest with his thumb.

The spectre raised his hands in frustration. 'Decades! Decades I waited! Planning my vengeance, waiting for it, longing for it. My only worry was this —' he pointed at the old man with his toe '— would die before I got my revenge.

'But he didn't, and here I am and you're not going to spoil it! Now kill him!'

I wondered how long it would be before a dozen students were at the door, trying to batter their way in, and how long it would be after that before the bolts gave way.

Not long, as it so happened. There were yells and oaths, the door began to shake. Thud, thud behind me. Both Finches looked at the door. The one lying down tried to yell for help.

'Enough,' muttered the ghost. 'We carry on as though you have free will, creature. But free will, like an afterlife, is largely illusory.'

I nodded. He was right, after all. I had come all this way: everything had conspired to bring me to this moment and to believe, now, that I enjoyed such a thing as free will was to surrender to the most stupid of illusions. Truly, I had never believed Finch's paper-thin arguments, but it had always been simpler to go along with them than to face responsbility. Because Finch wished it, the old man was going to die.

To be fierce, to be a killer! What else was there? To take refuge in revenge and rage. It felt good to be the ghost's creature, to obey him, and exult in it. This was what I was born for!

I raised the pistol, sighting along it with my good eye. The old man gasped, his lips trembled. Was he praying? A tear dropped down his cheek and I noted with disinterest that a dark wet stain was spreading across the cod of his breeches. The muzzle pointed at his chest. I squeezed the trigger.

There was a damp-sounding fizz, a flash of smoke. I looked at the old man, and he looked back at me, completely unharmed. The ball rolled out the end of the muzzle and hit the floor with a soft thud. Misfire.

The spectre groaned. 'Are you such an incompetent?'

The old man staggered to his feet, breathing heavily, while I stared at the useless pistol. He was yelling at the door, yelling to those outside to hurry or it would be all up with him. He had picked up a heavy statuette.

I reached into my coat for the other pistol.

The old man staggered towards me.

'How could I see Sinden?' he asked. 'What did you do to me?'

Sinden! A memory crashed like a sea-wave through a wall of glass. That was the spectre's real name! That's what the thing at the bottom of the well had called him!

I raised the pistol, pointing it at the old man.

He came on. The banging at the door grew louder.

I fired.

This time, there was no misfire. A flash, smoke and noise, and then there was the sound of something hitting the floor, wetly. The gunsmoke cleared, and I saw what I'd done.

The ball was not well-aimed. It must have clipped him on the side of the head, with much the same effect as a small hammer crashing down on one half of a soft-boiled egg. Some of the old man's head remained attached to his neck. The rest — blood, bone chips, brains, matted hair — was sprayed across the room. One leg was hooked under his body in an unnatural position. Oddly, I thought that it must be very uncomfortable for the old man to have to lie with his leg folded like that. For a moment, I thought of straightening the leg for him. Then my stomach caught up with my brain and I collapsed, vomiting.

The spectre, Sinden, laughed loud and hard as I crouched there on all fours, emptying the contents of my stomach on to the floor or up my nose. Even when there was nothing left, my stomach kept churning.

I am a killer.

Sinden laughed. 'I am avenged! Oh, it was worth the wait!' Out of the corner of my eye, I could saw him cut a caper. 'And the best part was, the old fool had no idea why you were going to kill him. Oh, pleased!'

There was a splintering sound. I guessed that one of the bolts had given way. Immediately after the gunshot, it had gone quiet outside, but then they'd redoubled their efforts. They continued to yell encouragement to Professor Finch and entreaties to the unknown assailant (me) not to harm the old man.

'And he really had to die?' I asked.

Sinden stopped his caper. 'Are you still here?'

I was not such a fool as to imagine that Sinden had ever intended to keep his promises. There was to be no reward, nor was there to be any escape for me. Sinden had got his revenge, and what happened to the weapon he had used was a matter of indifference. I would probably hang for this: but I wanted to know why.

'My goodness,' he said. 'There you are, still lying in your own vomit.

'Well, creature, don't worry too much. They'll be in soon and, when they see what you've done ... well ... it won't be pleasant, but it won't last long, I'm sure.'

'Tell me,' I said, 'just tell me.'

The spectre clicked his fingers and cocked an eyebrow. 'Tell you what?'

'Why. Tell me why you hated that old man so much.'

Sinden glanced at the corpse as though he'd already forgotten its presence. 'Who, him? I didn't hate him. Not especially, anyway. I just wasn't going to let him best me.

'I didn't lie when I said that revenge is all that's left when you're a ghost.'

Suddenly this all struck me as funny.

'I'm glad you can see the humour in this,' said the ghost, smirking. 'And, to tell you the truth, from my point of view it is rather funny. Anyway, thank you again. Goodbye.'

I looked down, my stomach cramping. Sinden was gone, and the door splintered and buckled as the students burst into the room. They saw what I'd done and then the beating began. I don't remember much of it, but they broke several ribs, most of the fingers in my left hand and my nose, and almost gouged out my remaining

eye. They clubbed me with my own pistols. Eventually some lictors
— porters with policing duties — arrived, and I was led away.

After the beating, the lictors gave me a few good kicks. And then
I was taken to this place, my cell, to await final sentencing. Professor
Finch was well-liked by his students and colleagues at the
Department of Philosophy, and even had a reputation in other parts
of the University for reliability and honesty. He was gentle with his
students but strict with miscreants. Even the likes of Margolis bowed
to him, looked up to him. So just about everyone who has had
a chance to do so has given me a clout or a thump or a kick.

They blindfolded me — twice as easy when the person to
be blindfolded has only half the number of eyes — and brought
me underground to the cells. I think there are other cells, perhaps
there's only this one. But really I have no idea because I am
completely alone. Not even Sinden, who was once Finch, has
visited me. Apart from my gaoler, I see no one.

The gaoler passes food to me in a bowl once a day, through
a hatch. There's a judas-hole in the door, with a cover on the other
side, so I can't look through it. But the gaoler can check in on me
anytime he wants. A pallet and a bucket for physical necessities
complete the furniture. No candles, no windows. I am not allowed
writing or reading material.

My chest and hand have been bound so that they will
become no worse, but no effort has been made to heal them. From
the few words I have exchanged with my gaoler, it's a forgone
conclusion that I'll be executed. There will be a trial. I may or may
not be allowed to attend. When I asked about a lawyer, the gaoler
laughed himself into a coughing fit and then spat in my soup.

There is no intention to wait for my injuries to heal before I am killed. Sensible.

I hope that Lucrese is not too disappointed in me. She will never know what went on, why I was in that room with Finch, why I killed him. She didn't see my brutality, and for that I'm grateful. She'll never know that I failed, that I never found out how to destroy Sinden.

Even now I think of Sinden as Finch. I knew him by the second name for too long to easily break the mental habit.

And really, how do I know that the ghost ever existed? It's entirely possible that I was battling with my own insanity. I think I might be mad, after all: mad with grief. Did I invent Finch-Sinden on the Isle of Goats, as a way to escape my suicide? Have I been wrestling with ghosts and demons in my own head, and nothing else? Did I kill an innocent man because I couldn't tell the real from the imagined?

There are hints of an inability to keep unreality in check: a particular pattern of cracks in the wall opposite, a whorl of sediment and a slight jut of stone have, in the interminable present since I was put here, gradually come more and more to look like Alexa. Soon it will be her face, and I will not be able to deny it.

I'm frightened of what will happen when Alexa appears here, with me. I don't want her to see what I have become. Killer of old men, attacker of women, coward and mad liar. Before that happens, I shall rise up and, even though there is no room in here to run, I will bash my head against the spot where she's forming. I'll bash my head against the spot, again and again and again, harder and harder. The stone will break skin, grazing my forehead and tearing out strands of hair that have been caught in cracks in the stonework. The pain will be awful; and I will continue, even as I see sparks with every thump, thump, thump.

Is it possible to kill myself in this way?

And so I continue to smash my head against this beautiful wall, which feels softer with every jolt. The soft, welcoming thuds as my blood trickles down my face, into my eyescarf, over my lips. But this hurts!

I don't remember when I stopped thinking about this and started doing it. Perhaps the dividing line between thought and deed is not so sharp, just like that between reality and fantasy.

I must be concussed by now. I try to bash my head against the wall once more and miss. As I slide into the darkness, down the wall, I remember that I have a lump on my cheeks, below my good eye, that Sinden gave me when he hit me. I did not imagine him.

Doors within me are unlocked, memories crash against the shore. I remember how I lost my eye.

THE UNDERMONSTER

A nd this is what I remembered.

Down I went, hungry and thirsty and enormously tired. The stairs below the Place of Dead Books spiralled back and around upon themselves. I kept going until my torch went out. I hadn't thought of that possibility when I left Vance and the others. I stopped dead, barely daring to breathe. And then my eyes adjusted: some light, a very little, filtered down the stairwell from the Library, far above. The walls themselves gave off a kind of greenish glow. Not much, but it was enough to avoid falling. Whether it was something in the rocks themselves, or some kind of lichen or fungus, I don't know. But I had light.

More, the walls were wet. Here and there were dark patches of moss, from which, I could just make out, water dripped down the walls. I sucked at every patch of moss I could find. It tasted strange, earthy and rusty, but was not distasteful. When you're thirsty, drinkable water always tastes sweet. It took a very long time, but drop by drop, moss patch by moss patch, I was able to get enough water.

I had been following the moss patches downwards: for how long, I can't say. I was now very deep beneath the Library. The air was dank. It's also possible that I slept for a while, either leaning against the wall or standing upright. I have vague, confused memories, such as could only come from dreams. And after a little I felt less tired, so perhaps I slept.

It may even be that I sleepwalked — down, of course — because my journey downwards ended when I blinked, or so it seemed to me, and instead of yet more of the monotonous spiral, there opened out in front of me an enormous flooded cavern. The walls, as far as I could see, were lined with that strange luminescence, and the dark water alternately reflected and absorbed the light as it rippled. The distance was a mild green haze.

A dark beach ran along the edge of the water. To my left it continued to the limits of vision, while to my right it ended at a confused jumble of rocks, a cliff. I sat down. I knew the way forwards but, once again, I needed to rest. I had been on my feet continuously for hours.

I knelt down and gazed into the dark water, at my reflection. Did I really resemble the ghost? Why could I not tell us apart? Did he exist only in my mind or, worse, did I exist only in his?

Out in the lake, something went plop.

I looked up. Something out there.

Then another plop, a little closer to me.

I fell back into a sitting position and scrambled a little way up the beach, away from the water.

A third plop. I saw something move.

I tried to get up, but suddenly my legs were so stiff that I simply flailed about. Rubbing hard to get some feeling into my thighs, I couldn't take my eyes off the little wave that showed something was heading towards me underwater. I had absolutely no doubts that whatever it was would be both carnivorous and amphibious. If the librarians here could be so dangerous, who knew what the fish were going to be like?

Then I thought of Vance and the others' fear of coming down here. They would rather run the gauntlet of the amok librarians than whatever it was I'd awoken.

My legs wouldn't work. I couldn't get up. My pistols! I grabbed them and rested them on my lap, fingers by the triggers.

Closer, now: there was a line of bubbles.

And then the top of it broke the surface of the water. Step by step it came towards me. I raised the first pistol and drew a bead on it.

It stayed crouched at the water's edge. It was like a man, but no man that I had ever seen before. It was all white, white like bleached paper, and hairless. It lacked nipples, a navel or genitalia. But otherwise its shape was unmistakably a fit, well-muscled man's. It was no more than four paces away, close enough to spring.

I raised my pistols. Let it have both barrels in the face!

'Hello,' it said, and I nearly dropped the pistols.

'You're on my beach,' it continued.

Its voice was strange. It seemed to speak in every accent I had ever heard, but yet with none of them. The voice sounded closer to me than the mouth which moved.

It blinked, and I did drop my pistols. Its eyelids were almost completely transparent. Only a slight opacity, flickering in front of its black irises (the only dark thing about it). Hastily, I picked my pistols up.

'I'll shoot,' I said. I didn't sound at all convincing.

The thing glanced at my flintlocks, and then its gaze stopped on me.

'The way your hands are shaking, I doubt that you'd hit me,' it said. 'Probably shoot yourself in the excitement. If you didn't accidentally kill yourself, I'd rip you long before you could reload those things.' And it yawned or grinned, showing a mouthful of long, sharp and translucent teeth. I was unpleasantly reminded of deep sea fish.

It yawned or grinned again. And blinked. I have never been so frightened. I may have whined.

'Can't move? Thinking we made a big mistake coming down here? Ever seen a fly in a spider's web? Can't move — doesn't know why.'

If I held one pistol with both hands, I could probably keep it steady enough to get a decent shot at the thing's head. Carefully, I laid one pistol on my lap and then steadied the other with my free hand. Lazily, the thing glanced at this arrangement and then back at my face.

'Oh, stop being silly! If I was going to hurt you, I would've done it by now.'

The flintlock wasn't shaking as much, but I still couldn't be sure of a clean shot. I doubted I would get a second one.

'No. I'm not going to harm you. I'm far more interested in that ghost that's been trotting around behind you.'

I dropped the pistol again. Oddly, it struck me as lucky that they didn't go off. Then I realised neither of them was cocked.

'Finch?' I whispered.

'Is that what he calls himself now? How interesting.' I can only describe its facial expression as a smirk.

'You know Finch?'

'Not by that name. But yes, I know "Finch".' The thing gazed off into the distance, then back at me. 'What are you doing with that spectre?'

What could I say to that? 'It wasn't my idea.'

The thing shrugged, then flattened itself. 'In such matters as these, it never is your idea. Tell me more about —' The creature stopped, raised its head as though listening. A moment later, there was a far off splash. The thing tensed, then stared at me. 'You'll have to excuse me,' it said, wiping its mouth with the back of one forearm, 'but it's feeding time.'

And then it flipped over, lithe as a seal, disappearing into the water with the vaguest of ripples.

Again, I tried to stand up. I could no longer feel my legs. I prodded them, slapped them, pinched. Nothing. They were limp and useless. It seemed that I had no choice but to wait here for the monster to return to finish me off. What had it said? Like a fly in a spider's web, the fly does not understand what holds it fast? Well, I could at least cock my flintlocks. This time I would make a good account of myself. I heard splashing out there, somewhere on the lake. After a while, it died down.

Some time later, the thing resurfaced.

'Hello again,' it said. I held my pistols ready, but didn't raise them.

'What are you?' I asked.

'Huh. I could as well ask the same of you. I don't go around with malevolent ghosts in tow.' It grinned, and its teeth were fearsome.

I waited.

'Well,' it said, at last, 'there are some who call me the undermonster.'

'And are you?'

Again, it grinned. 'Well, in a sense. But not all of the undermonster.' It paused, but I said nothing. It sighed. 'I am to the undermonster what your hand is to you. There? Does that help? I can't make it any clearer. Call me an avatar.'

I looked down at the pistols in my lap. Suddenly I knew: I had no chance of defeating this creature. It — the undermonster — was infinitely older and stronger and crueller than me, or even Finch. Foolish to think that I could try to protect myself with the flintlocks. It was all carnivorous, thwarted sensuousness and spinning, turning, eel-like hunger.

'And Finch?' I asked.

'Ah. Want to go for a swim?' The undermonster nodded back to the water. It yawned. 'No? I thought not.

'Well, regarding Finch — real name Sinden, in case this interests you — well, I'd like to know just what you think you're doing with him.'

I wanted to tell it. I wanted to confess my part in all this, in bringing Finch to the University, in being brought by Finch to the University. I wanted to explain that I was held by some power I didn't understand to do what Finch wanted, even though I knew it was wrong. I was a willing dupe in a game I didn't understand. Finch, or Sinden, or whatever he was, was in charge. I wanted to speak, but did not. I shook my head, helpless.

'Sinden isn't here, if that concerns you,' said the undermonster.

I couldn't believe that. Finch was always there, at my elbow. He chose to show himself only when we were alone. But he never left me. And he wouldn't until he had had his revenge.

'Well, even if you don't want to talk, I can promise you that Sinden isn't here. He won't come into my presence by choice.

He knows what will happen.' The undermonster glanced at the lake behind. 'Are you sure you won't go for a swim? The water's very clean … I keep it that way.'

I wondered what had hit the water before.

'I promise it's clean.'

I shook my head.

'No swim?' The undermonster looked sad. 'I won't eat you.' And then it gave me a sly, toothy look that said: 'Not yet, anyway.'

I still could not feel my legs.

'I'd like to be free of Finch,' I surprised myself. I did not think that I would be able to speak about it.

'Oh?' the undermonster waited.

'He wants to use me. I don't know what for, something about revenge. Somebody here hurt him. Killed him, perhaps.'

The undermonster made a gurgling noise, which I suppose passed for a chuckle.

'Well, nobody killed Sinden. Not here. But since he's obviously dead then somebody must have killed him out there — ' he waved, and the wave encompassed everything that was not the University '— after he left. By his own hand?' The undermonster looked at me, speculatively. 'Not you?'

'No,' I said.

'No. Too long ago.' The undermonster yawned.

'He must still be very angry. Well, Sinden never was one to put things in perspective! Talk about a temper.' The undermonster stretched, and scratched its neck. 'He's either very brave, or a fool. Probably a bit of both; they tend to go hand-in-hand.'

The undermonster rolled on its back, splashed at the water with its heels, and then rolled back onto its stomach.

'Listen,' it said, and its voice was deadly. 'I want you to bring Sinden here, to me. He and I have unfinished business. He must want his revenge very badly to run the risk of meeting me.'

'What can you do to him? He's a ghost.' Yet if the undermonster could harm Finch, perhaps I could after all be free of him.

The undermonster became very still. It raised its arms, and it spoke. 'To be dead is not the worst thing that can happen: to be dead is not sufficient to escape me. For Sinden to return, in whatever guise, is to open himself to the punishment that his infraction carries.'

'What punishment? What infraction?'

The undermonster looked into the distance. 'Sinden was exiled. He has returned, albeit dead. No matter. He broke exile and now he is mine.'

I had to know. 'What will you do to him?'

The undermonster looked taken aback. 'Do? Do? I'll eat him, of course.'

'A ghost. You'll eat a ghost?'

'There are stranger things. I am one of those stranger things.'

That I did not doubt.

'And me?' I did not wish to know the answer, but the question was out before I could stop myself.

'You?' the undermonster examined me, as though it had never seen me before and I was a mildly interesting specimen. 'I expect I'll eat you too. I eat most everybody around here, sooner or later.'

'Is everybody here punished, then?' I thought of Moira and despaired.

'It is not always a punishment.'

My head hurt. 'What is this place? What are you?'

The undermonster flicked back into the water. It swam in a circle, on its back, talking.

'I'm the end of the line. I'm where everything goes. For all production, there is destruction. I'm the "there is …" in that sentence. You make, I unmake. You create, I destroy. You mess things up, I tidy them.

'The tendency among you people is to assume that the act of creation is somehow morally in the ascendant over destruction. Pah!' The undermonster spun, disappeared and silently resurfaced by the water's edge. 'You could always come for a swim,' it bared its teeth.

Despite the undermonster's promise regarding my safety, I suspected that it was not entirely in control of its appetites. At least it didn't come fully onto the beach. I began to suspect it couldn't. The urge to crawl into the water, to bare my neck to its white lips and translucent teeth … 'Creation, destruction,' I prompted, hoping to break the spell.

It smacked its lips. 'Ah, yes. I'm forgetting my manners.

'I can tell you that creation is in no wise superior to destruction. You talk of creation and destruction, you all assume creation of works of art, and the destruction of said works. The artistic endeavour on one hand, and vandalism on the other. Yet my experience of humans is that, for the most part, you are no artists; instead, you create messes, problems, massacres, abortions and stinking piles of garbage. For every statue, a thousand miseries.

'I clean it up for you, and you think me a monster.' It held up one hand. 'I'm sorry, I have things to do. Back soon.'

The undermonster disappeared. A moment later, I heard splashing from far away. Lots of splashes. And perhaps a thin, high scream. I shuddered. Hell must be not unlike this place, except I would expect Hell to make more sense.

After a while, the splashing died down. I waited for the undermonster to return, feeling relatively safe on the spit. Within a few minutes, it was again half-beached a little way from my feet.

'Where was I?' it began.

'How do I bring Finch to you?' I interrupted.

It glared at me. 'Oh, you'll know,' it said, airily.

'But he's a ghost.'

Slowly, as though to an idiot or small child, it said, 'Just grab him and bring him to me. I'll take care of the rest.'

'How do I grab a ghost?'

The undermonster ignored my question. 'I am the answer. Do you know what the question is?'

I shook my head.

'The question is, "How do you grab a ghost?"' The undermonster kicked its heels and made that gurgling, chuckling sound. I was nauseated. I was watching a moray eel wear a party hat.

And then it pounced.

I tried to roll away, raising a pistol, but already it was upon me, knocking the pistol away almost lazily. It held me down by the shoulders and yet still held my head still, hard hands on my cheeks. How many arms did this thing have?

It grinned, its cold nose touching mine. Then its mouth closed over my right eye. I screamed in pain and fear. It sucked, hard. I won't try to describe what it felt like or what I saw with that eye before it was sucked from its socket.

The undermonster let go and I, sobbing and bleeding, surely dying, fell back into darkness. I saw it smile and there was no mercy or pity in the smile. Only malice towards the universe and a complete indifference to me.

'Yes,' it said, and its voice was sad. 'I'm monstrous. But there are worse things to be than that.'

———————

Up from the darkness I swam: up, up — from the cool and soothing dark and into the world of light and pain. I blinked, and the pain across the right side of my face seared. I coughed, and again the pain lanced across my cheek, my ruined face. I shut my left eye — the right eyelid seemed to be already gummed shut — and lay quite still. After a while, when I had built up the courage, I raised my hand to my face. I felt the caked roughness, the telltale of dried blood on my cheek. I must have bled quite profusely. And then, gingerly, I brushed my eyelashes with just the tips of my fingers. They were matted together, stiff. Ever so gently, I sought further. It hurt, as expected, but I did not pull my hand away. I felt almost no skin; the whole of where my right eye used to be and the cheek were a giant clot.

How long had I been lying here?

More to the point, why was I not dead?

For a moment it seemed the only thing to do would be to find one of my pistols and finally, and not before time, lodge a musket ball in my brain. But the urge passed, and even with only one eye I desired life too much to die.

Gently, ever so gently, I laid my palm flat against the clot. I wanted to open my good eye, and I was worried that the involuntary movement of my bad eye's lid might tear the clot, start the bleeding again. The palm pressed against the right side of my face created a strange kind of reassurance, and I opened the other eye.

I lay where I must have passed out after the undermonster attacked me. Cold and miserable. Sorry for myself, too, but that's nothing new. Looking around in the half-light, I saw my pistols on the ground. I rose and, still holding my eye shut, retrieved them. One I jammed down my belt, the other I held. If the undermonster returned for the other eye, I wanted to get in at least one good shot first.

I can't stay here. I'd die here.

Which way? This way: the other way was a dead end.

Considered from a certain perspective, life itself is a dead end.

Limping forward, I settled into a shuffling rhythm, where each step jolted my wound. I whimpered a little, but kept going forward. And forward. Another step, and then another. Try not to think of the undermonster, of those teeth. Just keep going. Another step.

When did my legs start working again?

And further ahead I saw a stone jetty. Tied halfway along was a small rowboat. As I neared the jetty, I knew without needing to think of it that I would limp out along it, crawling the last few steps, and then tumble into the dinghy. I cracked my head when I hit the thwart and dropped one of my pistols into the bottom of the boat, but I managed to keep holding my eye shut.

I think I must have slept for a while: I felt a little stronger, strong enough to reach forward and untie the dinghy from its mooring. It drifted ever so slightly in the almost motionless water, tapped against the jetty once and twice, and then I fell asleep again.

When I awoke, it seemed at first that the boat was motionless, but then I felt a very slight rocking, and from the breeze against my cheek, I sensed the boat was moving. Quite rapidly, too. Perhaps this is another dream: I'm sure that at some time the dinghy passed an ancient sailing ship, covered in cobwebs and seemingly stuck in the water like a fly in amber. At another time I imagined the undermonster was in the boat with me. It was quite friendly and explained that I should not regard the underlake as being enclosed by the University. Rather, the reverse is true: the University is an island. Or not an island, something else. Different, but similar. It apologised for my eye but said I'll understand.

Later, I lay with my head in its lap. It stroked my hair and, bent across me, sang gibberish. In the song, all words were merely arbitrary pointers that could just as well point to something else, anything else, nothing at all: if 'chair' could mean a boot and if 'up' could really be 'down' and vice versa, then how can we communicate at all? The chorus was something about passing another bottle. I tried to join in but my mouth felt full of wool. Apparently I was sucking on my tricorn hat which, despite all expectations, was still with me.

This all within a mist composed of empty books and pregnant lakes that have never seen sunlight. I despair.

After another lifetime, the boat fetched up against a beach. I think lazily that I must have been travelling very fast because the boat completely left the water. I don't know how I know that. Blood or something else trickled warmly down my cheek. I can see a cloud, the sun. And then my one eye rolled back into my head and I didn't know anything anymore.

MY EXECUTION

They woke me by splashing water in my face. Spluttering, my head aching and my face stinging, I was pulled into a sitting position and then upright. Hands brought to the front, my wrists were tied together. Somebody asked what I had done to get into this state. Vaguely, I understood that the speaker was asking about me, not speaking to me directly.

Had I really killed a harmless old man? What sort of monster was I?

I looked around. I was in what I took to be the corridor outside my cell. Four men surrounded me, all wearing black robes and black masks. Executioners.

'So it's death, then?' I murmured, only slightly interested in the question or the answer.

'Shut yer yap,' said one of them.

Another shushed him. 'It's not good to treat a dead man like that,' he said. Then to me: 'I'm sorry to tell you, you've been found guilty of murder.'

I smiled. I was going to die. I felt very little, except tired and somewhat dizzy. And the headache from my bashing my head against the wall was a constant.

They blindfolded me. I felt a moment of fear. I didn't want to die unknowing, clubbed to death halfway down some anonymous corridor with my face covered. I wanted to be prepared. 'I won't die blindfolded, will I?'

'No. You'll get the chance to see your end, if that's what you want.'

Stumbling, a rope about my neck, I was led through dripping and forgotten passages. How long we walked, I have no idea: distances within the University always seem long. I was forever amazed at just how much space was contained within its walls. And up staircase after staircase we went. Ascending to the skies, or so it seemed.

After a while, I could hear noises ahead. A crowd, restless and waiting with little patience. I could smell them, smell their desire for my blood.

A change in the quality of light and the smell of the air suggested to me that we were coming out into an open area. And then there was no doubt, as I felt a breeze and heard the crowd yell. There were a couple of hundred people here, witnesses to ensure that the execution went off as expected. They could then report to their various areas, or whatever it was they each represented.

Over and above it all, I heard the crows cawing. I wondered how I came to be in this mess, yet I felt no self-pity. I was too tired of it all, too tired of myself, to feel sorry for me or to worry about my end.

A tug on the rope from behind, and I halted. One of my captors removed the blindfold. They were too rough doing it and removed my eyescarf as well. So my ugly, scarred face was bared completely. I began to say something, then left it. No matter.

I stood on a very slightly raised platform. Something about the movement of air behind me, and especially at my ankles, gave me the idea that I stood with my back to a cliff, one quite close. So that I was how I was to die: tossed or jumping from a cliff, and me afraid of heights. There was a kind of barbarism in that form of execution which surprised me. I would not have thought the University to do things in quite this way. The noose or the firing-squad would, I thought, be more appropriate. To ensure that I did not spoil the proceedings by flinging myself off too soon, the captors held my shoulders and the rope about my neck.

We were on an open space which must have been at the top of one of the highest towers. The wind was fresh and strong, carrying with it the tang of the sea. To my left and right were tiered seats, packed with venerable-looking men and women; academics, for the most part. There were some younger ones; student representatives, I guessed. I saw Margolis in the crowd, watching me with a studied fascination. Did she suddenly find me attractive now that I was a killer, I wondered: a kind of man she'd never encountered before. I couldn't see Lucrese, and decided she was not present — for that I was grateful.

Directly in front of me was a high desk, rising above my head. Behind it sat three men and two women. Of these, I recognised only the Aardvark, who sat at one end with a quill in hand. He was picking his nose and conducting minute examinations of the extracted debris before wiping it on his robe. The others were dressed in habits of the deepest blue silk, a colour so close to black it was only in the folds, where the play of light was subtly different, lightening it, that the real hue was apparent. All of them wore powdered periwigs in the style of a generation or more ago. The youngest one was the Aardvark, and he was a man advanced in years. Directly in front of the high desk was a lit brazier guarded by a pair of lictors.

The tiered seats and the high desk in front of me were constructed of wood. Although solidly built, they had that air of being temporary structures. They had been put together for my benefit, then. Probably they broke down for easy storage, to be brought out when needed. What events other than executions justified their use? And this area, at the top of a truncated tower, what was it used for at other times? Perhaps nothing.

One of the women leaned across to the man seated in the centre of the group and whispered something. He nodded, raised his hand. Somewhere, a drum beat once and twice. The crowd's yelling died to a murmur and then to almost nothing.

'Is this the prisoner?' asked the man in the centre of the group.

The Aardvark turned to him: 'Aye, it is, your honour.'

The presiding judge — that's what I assumed him to be — nodded and grunted. He cleared his throat.

'Very well,' he began, in a clear and strong voice, 'know then, that we are here assembled to carry out sentence on the prisoner, who has been found guilty of murder of the beloved Professor Josef Finch, lately of the Philosophy Department of the University.

'Know further, that this sentence shall be carried out here, today. It will also be observed by the Chancellor of the University, who is watching from his tower.' Here, the presiding judge motioned towards a spot somewhere behind me, in the air.

Then I saw Sinden. The spectre strolled around from behind the dais, through a space between it and the tiered seats to my right.

He was watching me, a half-smile on his face, and his hands behind his back. There was something about the way he walked, the way he looked, that gave me a strange idea. It seemed to me that he thought I could not see him, just as the others could not see him. On a hunch I lifted my bound hands to my missing eye.

At the first movement from me, the presiding judge stopped speaking. He'd been reciting from memory a list of precedents for what they were about to do. Apparently there had been quite a few murders in the University's history, mostly ending with an execution of the guilty party — or someone who seemed guilty enough for the purpose.

'The prisoner will be restrained,' muttered one of the other judges. One of my captors reached forward and brought my hands back to the front. Just before they did that; however, I managed to cover my missing eye's socket with my hands. And as I did so, the spectre disappeared. When my hands were pulled down, I could see him again.

I wanted to laugh out loud, but dared not: so I could see Sinden. He thought he was invisible to me. That I saw him out of a non-existent eye did not strike me as in the least paradoxical. If anything, it made a kind of strange sense. To see the invisible, look without eyes. Had the undermonster known what it was doing when it took my eye? Was that, perhaps, the purpose of the mutilation? I realised that I could have seen Sinden at any time after my encounter with the undermonster, if I had simply taken off my eyescarf. Because Sinden had never left my side. Ever since the Isle of Goats, he'd been near, except when I was in the undermonster's lair. He only chose to let me see him when it suited him.

I remembered the Best of All Possible Worlds in Margolis' rooms. When I had finally been able to see into that world, it had been because I'd absent-mindedly put my missing eye to the eyepiece. And I hadn't realised it until now.

Since Sinden could not know that I was able to see him, I had, at last, an advantage. It was important that I didn't let the ghost realise I could see, truly see, so as to retain my advantage until I knew how to use it.

'And so,' droned the presiding judge, 'by all legal precedents and by the laws of morality, our action is just.'

He had spent a half hour citing legal precedent, but then simply skimmed over the moral side of the question with a nod, as though to something distasteful. It struck me that the legal profession at the University was no different to what I'd encountered elsewhere.

'And so the sentence will be carried out,' said the judge.

Sinden stood below the dais. He was shaking with laughter.

'First, your queue is to be cut off, and thrown into a fire.'

One of the lictors guarding the brazier pulled out a pair of shears from his habit.

'Then, you are to be thrown off this tower.'

There was a pause. I imagined the long, long fall. What would happen to my body? On what would I crash? I thought of burst intestines and heads like broken melons, the old professor after I shot him.

'Lictor, remove the prisoner's queue.'

The lictor walked up behind me and cut off the sign of my male adulthood. He carried it back to the brazier and dropped it in the fire. There was a crackle and the smell of burning hair. Sinden watched, fascinated. Then he walked across the empty space to stand next to me. I dared not look at him.

If Sinden could touch me, then perhaps I could touch him. Could I grab him and take him with me? The fall was fatal for someone of flesh and blood: would it harm a ghost?

The presiding judge continued. 'I commend your soul to the heavens and your body to the underlake.'

Snap. It was as though a missing piece in a jigsaw puzzle — the last section of sky — had been found and placed. The fall behind me did not end with a splat on rocks, it ended under the University, in the lair of the undermonster. That's what they did with their murderers, just as that was how they buried their dead. The dead and those who should be dead were fed to the undermonster.

If I could get a hold on Sinden and take him with me, then I would deliver him to the undermonster. That would be the way to kill the spectre. I would die, too, but I did not fear it because I was not thinking about my own death. Only Sinden's. And afterwards, perhaps I would have earned the privilege of being reunited with Alexa.

The presiding judge opened his mouth, to order the lictors to throw me over the edge.

Sinden was yet too far from me.

'Wait,' I said, straightening up as much as my injuries would let me, 'am I not permitted a last word?'

The judges turned to each other, the presiding judge with one hand half-raised. They turned back to me.

'No,' he said.

I lowered my head. The decorum of the moment was lost by my interruption. The judges huffed and straightened their robes, one tugged at the end of his periwig.

Sinden had taken the bait. Thinking there was something more that I wanted to say, perhaps wanting to feel my body warmth one last time, he crept to my side. Then he bent over, trying to divine something from my attitude. I looked straight into his eyes. His smile vanished as he realised that I could see him. Shock, fear; and then he jumped away.

I'm not a man of action. Generally, I'm rather clumsy, a bereaved clerk in a strange situation.

I leapt at him, just as the presiding judge was saying: 'Lictors, carry out the sentence.'

I raised my bound hands and formed a loop with my arms, falling on him as he moved away. He didn't move fast enough. It was only a step between us and then my arms came down around his shoulders like a hoop, pinning his arms to his sides.

He was cold. It was like hugging a block of ice.

He hissed at me.

The rope around my neck went taut and I was jerked back.

Sinden began to wriggle free as the judge yelled at the lictors to stop me from getting away, but they all misunderstood where I was trying to go.

If I didn't go over the edge soon, Sinden would duck under my arms and away from me: he had free movement of his legs, whereas the lictors were trying to immobilise me.

To break free I spun, using the momentum of my guards on me to fling myself and Sinden towards the edge. I was too busy to think about the edge, about the fall.

Sinden's eyes widened even further.

We spun around, a crazy dance.

People were yelling, screaming. This wasn't the way events should unfold!

The guard holding the rope must have dropped it, because it went slack.

The dance continued, and then there was no ground to dance on.

Sinden wriggled like a snake. 'You bastard!' he yelled. My arms ached. It seemed to me that the skin must be sloughing off, burnt with the cold.

I smiled at the spectre.

I couldn't breathe too well. I had so many broken bones, both ribs and those in my hand. And they were all complaining as Sinden pushed against me, trying to find some point of weakness.

But as we fell, we were on an equal footing, and he could not escape.

As the wind screamed past us, I saw the tops of towers loom up and then zip past, needles of stone.

I wasn't frightened. I was too focused on holding the ghost to me to worry about what came next. And truly, it was of no matter to me that I was about to die. I felt immensely tired of life. Drawing breath was an agony, and a boring one: time to see Alexa, if such a thing were permitted. Time to see my child. Life was not so immensely sweet that it was acceptable under any and all conditions.

'Free me, creature!'

We seemed to have been falling a long time. It grew darker, and now we fell surrounded by wet stone.

I laughed in Sinden's face. Too sore to speak. Couldn't the spectre see he had no power any more?

More stone.

And then we fell through an open space. The undermonster's cavern.

I had thought that, when I hit the water, it would break my neck. That would be all for me, and then Sinden could be safely left to the mercies of the undermonster. But the water did not turn out to be the hard landing I expected. We broke through, and went under, deep and deeper.

How deep is it? I wondered. The shock of impact had punched all the air out of my lungs. My body was a wall of agony in which I was encased. I couldn't move, couldn't breathe. And then my wits returned. I was slowly rising in the water, my hands spreadeagled. The impact must have broken my bonds. Either way, Sinden was gone.

I didn't have the courage to drown myself here, alone, in the black water. Painfully, my broken hand complaining with every stroke, I swam to the surface.

And then I was floating.

Although it hurt to breathe, I gulped in the air. I wanted to die, but not quite yet.

'Why won't you die?' It was Sinden.

I turned in the water. He was floating a few metres from me. For a ghost, he seemed pretty sluggish in the water.

I waved to him, cheekily, still panting. 'You're a spectre, Sinden. Why don't you rise and float away? Isn't that what ghosts do?'

Everything went blurry for a moment. Yelling at him had taken most of my energy.

Sinden spluttered, cursing. He swam towards me, clumsily. Perhaps in life he'd been a poor swimmer, whereas I was moderately confident in the water. Even so, in my current state I couldn't move with anything like the speed that I would need to escape him.

He was angry, but frightened, too: he knew where he was, and what sort of danger he was in. As the undermonster had said, there were dues to be paid.

The water behind Sinden grew white, as though lit from below. Sinden stopped swimming, his eyes wide. The light increased in intensity. The spectre looked at me in terror, mouth agape.

Something broke the surface behind Sinden. Something white and hairless, with a shape not unlike a human's. With long translucent teeth, hungry and fast.

Moving like a dart, it reared up behind Sinden. He looked up, his eyes rolled so far that I could not see much more than the whites. He didn't have time to scream before it plunged and closed around him. The water churned. A slight wave caught me and, in a panic, I struck out away from where the undermonster was settling unfinished business.

I swam, painfully, on my back, for a few minutes. As the noises subsided, I struck something hard but strangely pliant. Reaching behind me, I felt a tangle of ropes. I looked up, and saw the side of a ship, a rope ladder draped like a net for seamonsters along its length. I had passed this ship, or thought I had, in my delirium after the undermonster took my eye.

With appalling slowness, I hauled myself up the ladder, backwards. I didn't want to take my eyes off the water. Eventually, I raised myself out as far as the tops of my legs. That was enough. Arms hooked through the rope ladder, I waited for the undermonster to come for me.

I did not have to wait long. Soon enough, I saw a white shape flickering close to the surface, some way off. Once or twice it broke water, then stopped and surfaced up to its chest, about three metres from me.

I felt no fear, just a mild distaste. I was too tired and too pained to feel anything much else.

The undermonster raised its hand in salute. 'Well, that's that, then.'

I waited. Soon, teeth and bone.

It floated along on its back, kicking lazily. 'He was a nasty piece of work, that one. Nasty. Philosophers always taste of bile and envy.'

It stopped, watching me.

'And what of you?' it asked.

I looked up. 'I want to die.'

'Oh.' It shook its head. 'We all want to die.'

'But I killed that old man. There's still my punishment.'

'There's a common misconception that my role in all this is to do the bidding of them upstairs,' the undermonster flicked its head to indicate the roof of the cavern. 'Nonsense, really. I exist as one end of an axis. The University revolves around that axis.'

The undermonster disappeared, and then resurfaced at my feet.

'I think I'll let you live.' It smiled, and its smile was mirthless. 'And I'm not going to eat any other part of you, not this time.'

They thought I would die down with the undermonster. When I returned, bruised and battered and nearly broken, they said it was a bloody miracle that I was still alive. So I was released, because if the undermonster considered me worthy of life, then life I must have.

I did not know where to go or what to do, now that I was free of Finch and Sinden. I could have returned to my home city, but I had no more reason to do that than I'd had for staying in it in the first place.

I stayed in the Sanatorium while my bones knitted. The others were still there. At first they remained standoffish; after all, I was a convicted murderer. But they longed to hear the story, and over oranges and between breaks in Arcane Starfish, I told them all about it, about the murder and my madness, and the undermonster. But I did not tell them about Sinden. They assumed that in killing old Professor Finch, I was doing the undermonster's bidding. And by neither affirming nor denying that interpretation, I allowed it to become the truth. It was the story that spread into the University and became the accepted version of the story of my execution and resurrection.

When I was healed sufficiently, I went back to Lucrese and she welcomed me back to her bed. She did not understand what had happened, and did not ask — for which I was glad — but it was an unspoken understanding between us that I had slain my demon. We never parted. She became my second wife and I cannot say that our life together was unhappy, although we never had a child. She saw me with open eyes, although she did not comprehend everything she saw. And I must say that the same is true of me: I saw her for what she was, but what she was, I can't really say, except that she was kind and honest to a painful degree.

I went back to my position with the Department of Information, but Professor Margolis feared me. Perhaps for the first time in her life, she had encountered someone more monstrous than she. I terrified her, and the reverse was no longer true. I was promoted out of her sphere of influence, something which

I suspect she may even have had a hand in. I rose away instead of falling off a balcony.

Thirty years have passed. Promotion has followed promotion and my rise in the University bureaucracy has been rapid. Eventually, I became Principal Private Secretary to the Chancellor. He is an ancient man, easily more than a hundred years old, perhaps more than two hundred. He 'lives', if that's the word, in a bath chair. His physical needs are attended to by a group of similarly ancient doctors. He eats many oranges. He never ventures from the top rooms of the highest tower in the University. And it is here that, every day, I meet with him in conference and pass on his orders for the running of the place.

The Chancellor sits and broods and refuses to change anything. It is his wish, communicated by slow gestures, for the University to stay exactly as it is, exactly as it has always been. Since I became his Principal Private Secretary, it's become apparent to the rest of the University that the Chancellor, or someone close to him, is having fresh ideas. Some have involved improved efficiency in dealing with student applications, or in bringing to heel the members of certain departments. Most notably, a strange mariner's globe was removed from the Department of Information and placed in the safekeeping of the newly-formed University Museum. Additionally, the position of Principal Private Secretary to the Chancellor has been vested with a great many more powers, and a small but efficient staff.

I discovered that the opposite end of the axis to the undermonster is the Chancellor. Now, I am the intermediary of that end of the axis with the rest of the world. Every day I feel the tugging of the undermonster and between us, the University continues its daily, weekly, yearly round.

I have been in the presence of the Chancellor many times. He is ancient, like dust and ancestral hate. Perhaps he was once a young man, perhaps even a baby at his mother's breast, but I cannot believe this. Now he is a tiny creature, a shrivelled ball of ineffectual spite in a bath chair. He chews his mash very slowly, using false teeth carved from oak, and sometimes blinks. Every hour, on the hour, he takes a shallow breath. He is attended by six liveried servants who do not blink, do not breathe, do not reply to any but the orders of their master. Every morning, a maid arrives with a large key which she inserts, one by one, into the small of their backs. After she has wound them up, they are ready for their duties.

The Chancellor's chambers were once brightly furnished, but the cloth-of-gold and silks have all faded to a flat, washed-out nothing. So ancient are the hanging cloths and furniture that sudden gusts of wind tear off corners. So no wind is allowed in the Chancellor's rooms. There is almost no movement, almost no sound, except for the dull ticking from the six valets' mechanical hearts.

The Chancellor's rooms, being higher than all other buildings, higher even than the flight paths of the condors that feed on the crows, has a magnificent view of all the lands about. I love to look through the Chancellor's eyeglass at the sea beyond the headlands. Occasionally I spot white flashes, sails, far off out there, and I wonder what lands lie beyond. Over the years I have read of many strange and marvellous places in books I've borrowed from the Library, but I have also learnt that all books lie.

For the rest, there is little to tell. I have grown older in the service of the University, have grown into my power. I have passed through middle age, and I see old age approaching. I wonder, sometimes, whether I have not outlived my own life. Perhaps I should have died, years ago, with Sinden.

Lucrese died last year, and I am now twice a widower. I miss her, even though in her final years she lost her mind and control of her body. I and her colleagues, the doctors, we nursed her until she died. To know her was greater luck than I deserved.

Sharkey, mad for scaffolds and miserable behind a desk, with a body made for clambering and moving and lifting, but with a trepan-plate in his skull that made scaffolds a forbidden land — well, he hung himself. I know this because all deaths are reported to the Chancellor's office before it is permitted to send them to the underlake.

Enthusiastic participation in the occasional riots and orgies of the librarians did not impede Moira's career. She rose to be in charge of the Reference Section, and then married a senior librarian whose tastes in the bedroom extended to the strange. I have my sources throughout the University and I understand that she rather enjoyed it. Eventually, her husband died of the cryp.

And almost every day through the spyglass I watch Polk, out there in the village of Drab. No longer a village but a small town, and he is its mayor. Mary and he have many children, and two grandchildren. Moneys have been disbursed, over the years, from the University coffers at the behest of the Chancellor's Principal Private Secretary to assist in projects to improve the amenity of Drab. So there are irrigated fields, a real fishing fleet, even a small school. There are oranges, distributed to the children at school. Polk and Mary and Drab have prospered, but they've worked hard for it. The town no longer relies on the University for its survival.

I don't know if this could be called a happy ending. It's just an ending, insofar as anything short of death is an ending.

EPILOGUE:
WITH SAILS UNFURLED

Past are the hours and days, weeks and months, years and years and years. I have walked these boulevardes and halls and quadrangles, I have stood on these balconies, I have watched students pass beneath the walls. I have received their honours, played the politics, sent out my spies. I have learnt by patient application that it is true, as Finch said, that the University has its own rhythms and patterns, and that the life of a single mortal is not long enough to discern more than a fragment. I have been to the kitchens, once, and of that I will not speak. In all this time, I have only ever seen sunshine at a distance, from beyond the fringe of the dark clouds that unceasingly hover above the University. Sometimes, I have been down as far as the outskirts of Drab, and felt the warmth of breezes from beyond the grey zone, but seeing to my duties has meant that I could never travel far enough away from the University's shadow to feel the sun on my face or on the backs of my hands.

I am in my private quarters, surrounded by the accumulations of my life. These rooms are spacious and comfortable, I have maids and a valet to see to my needs. The rooms and the servants are the best that the University can provide. There is a bowl of fruit on an occasional table, bookcases full of the finest literature ever produced by the University: great thinkers and feelers. Sometimes, with a start, I remember that there, beyond the University, a whole world exists. We have little discourse with them, up here in this tower. We don't need them and, I suspect, they do not need us.

I walk past the books, across the ancient rug, fine-woven with silver, out onto the stone balcony, second highest in the University, second only to the Chancellor's. I am but a floor below the Chancellor, ready at all times to assist him, for that is my first and only official duty. Below me, the campus stretches out, a maze of stone and wood, sickly grass and ever-dying trees. I hear the vague murmur, like a sigh or bees far off, dreamily, that is the sum total of all the activities that are the University, the University going about its business. Somewhere, down there, new thoughts and ideas are being born. Elsewhere, the young are learning, being taught things that may or may not be of any use to them before they are sent back to the lands from whence they came, to forget us, except when they are middle-aged and drunk, and then we will be remembered in a nostalgic longing for a half-lived youth. Then they shed oily tears for the old place. And in a million wooden frames across the campus, worms are devouring; in books everywhere, ideas are failing and dying; among the people there are births and deaths, trusts placed and trusts betrayed.

The ancients understood that one should never outlive one's life. Sometimes they described the moment as being tired of life; at other times, as outliving one's own time or outliving one's own usefulness. I think that I understand that feeling. I'm tired. I'm an old man, my kidneys ache and my legs are bandy. I don't see so well. Too many people that I know are now counted among the dead, and I burn incense to their honour. All the living in this place, except the Chancellor, seem interchangeable and soft-faced, like dough let out of the oven too soon.

I have two last debts to pay. I killed a man, and I ruined another's hopes. It seems to me that I must atone for these acts; or more accurately, that a lifetime of trying to atone has not been enough.

There's one more thing that I must do, and then my usefulness is at an end.

Here is the portrait of Lucrese, that I have kept on my desk in the Chancellery for decades. She has been dead, now, longer than we were married. It was her self-honesty and refusal to have any illusions that inspired me, surrounded as I was for years by the venality of office intrigue. A Chancellor's staff are no different to any other group of people, always manoeuvring for power or distinction. I stroke her hair with my finger, but all I feel is faded oil paint against canvas, slightly rough. I have to hold the picture close to my eye, at an angle to maximise the light falling across it, so that I can see her at all, so dim has my vision become. One last view before I pass it into the fire. For a moment it sits there on the coals, the fire seemingly surprised by this intrusion. Then, the frame chars and separates, the ancient oil bubbling and coming to life as the canvas curls. Now the frame is burning strongly. Goodbye, Lucrese.

It occurs to me that I had another wife, before Lucrese. I don't remember her name, or what she was like. That was long ago, in a previous life, or a life that happened to a different man. I whisper goodbye to her, too, whoever she was.

And then I drop a small square of tanned hide onto the fire. It's part of the skin of a dead mule that was found by my spies in a long-forgotten garden. It may have been the only mule to ever escape the kitchens: I do not know if it was my old mule, but I like to think so.

In a locked box there is a slim volume, bound in cloth sealed with a leather clasp. I hold it once again, for the last time. The total of a life, it's a small book, easily held in one hand. The total of his life, held in my hand. A monograph on the nature of useless things. Except, of course, that nothing is useless in its time. Poor Sinden, I have grown fond of him. After he ceased haunting me, his memory softened and became more sympathetic. I know it's a lie, a trick of the light and of age, but I prefer to remember him as a noble sufferer, one undone by fate and his own nature, a nature so extreme that even death could not hold him back from his revenge. Although years of political street fighting have made me otherwise, at the time I knew him I was weak, easily controlled by others. What chance could I ever have had against a personality as strong as Sinden's? Not even the laws of prudence could bind him: he disregarded what would almost certainly happen to him if he returned to the University, alive or dead. He was willing to be destroyed in order to have revenge — had it not been me, sooner or later someone would have served him up to the undermonster.

And in the years since then, I have, through patient interviewing of those old enough to remember, and through sending my underlings scouring through the Library and the archives, learned why it was that Sinden wanted revenge so badly. It was nothing more complicated than being thwarted: Sinden sought a lectureship, and a woman, and he was beaten to both by Finch. The joke being, of course, that Finch was not even aware that he was in competition with Sinden for either. But Sinden knew, and the knowledge ate him up, because he could not stand ever to be bested. He was not a man to ever bow, accept defeat, smile, acknowledge that the better man won. And in a rage, he flew at the woman, whose name isn't important but was Julia.

He injured her. How, I don't know, but I understand it was not possible for her to bear children. For that, he was banished from the University, only to return on pain of death. He travelled as far as the Isle of Goats and there hung himself. So I burn incense to his memory, and to Julia's, who I did not know.

Apart from the one instance of Sinden, I have never had any reason to suspect, no hint, that there is any survival after death. I no longer believe in the ancestors. My incense-burning is an act of memorial.

I toss the book into the flames. After a while, the paper sears and the cloth binding dissolves in a blue flame. The pages will slowly smoulder. Perhaps I should have torn them out first. Oh well, it's too late now.

My queue has long since regrown. The hairs are grey, turning white. I reach up behind my head and hold the queue taut with one hand while I cut it off with shears held in the other. I glance at it, but the things of myself hold little interest. It goes in the fire and, for the first time in many years, I smell my own hair burning.

There's nothing else of interest or of value in this room. The relics and reminders of all that mattered to me have been burned. I have sundered my connection with this place. There is a note at my writing-desk, explaining the reasons for my departure and wishing my staff farewell. My valet will find it later today, when he comes to receive my orders for dinner. I have given strict instructions that I am not to be disturbed until then.

With a lantern and a rope in a sack, I leave my home for the last time. I would not say that I strode out, as though owner of all the world; but then I didn't exactly creep, either.

Down the stairs I go, down and down. Every hour or so, I stop on a landing to catch my breath and stretch my back. Age has wearied me. Then on I go, often leaning on the banister for support. The Chancellery tower has an internal staircase, unconnected with the daily commerce up and down the outer stairs, that leads directly to the underlake.

Outside the walls, beyond my vision, I pass the tops of the other towers. Then the bodies of the high buildings, the great halls. Past lectures and tutorials, learned disquisitions and debates. Past painters and writers, farriers and blacksmiths, cooks and char ladies. Past lecturers and dons, scholars and readers, dogs and cats. On I go, down I go. Past trees, grass, columns and bookshelves. Past the hidden bodies and carnal encounters. Down past rats and beetles. Past, finally, the innermost circle of the Library, which I know is empty, completely devoid of books. Below that, the Place of Dead Books. Down to the waterline, the cavern of the undermonster.

As the Principal Private Secretary to the Chancellor, it's important that I know of the existence of this staircase. It's also important that I should never use it: it is reserved only for the Chancellor himself. But the Chancellor is nearly three hundred years old, and close to death. The struggles among those who think they might replace him, and their factions, are becoming deadly. What started as sniping with words will end with poison and duels. The Chancellor is dying, and I am his right hand. So I consider it my right by proxy to use this staircase, for the first and last time.

I'm surprised where the stone staircase ends: on the deck of that ancient ship that I have seen twice before.

As I approach the hull, I feel the staircase sway and bend, inasmuch as stone can give. There's a sense of longing for movement here, a strumming of harp strings. Closer to the deck, and I see the mounds of cobwebs and dust, mixed over centuries with the moist salt air to form great piles of a semi-light, sticky sludge. I shudder when I touch it, but it's impossible to avoid, since it reaches several turns up the staircase. It feels clammy, clingy.

Through the stuff I see at least a dozen shapes that, despite age and the obscuring veils of cobwebs, are still all too recognisable, clad in faded blue habits that I feel I should recognise, but can't. No matter, it is not with these desiccated mummies that I have come to deal.

Gingerly, I walk to the side of the ship, and gaze into the dark water below. I don't have long to wait. There's a flicker, then another, then a small wave near the hull. Then a familiar white head bobs up. How often have I seen this in nightmares?

'Hello,' it says.

I wave back, trusting that it can see me, even though to my old eye it is only a blur.

'Why are you here?' Is it possible the undermonster does not know everything?

'I've come to see you.'

'Ah.' It pauses, disappears under the water, then reappears a few metres away. 'Why?'

I had expected it to drag me in immediately. Should I throw myself into the water, trusting that it will be quick?

'We've unfinished business.' What else can I say?

It disappears under the water again. This time, it comes up by the ship's hull, darting up the rope ladder until it's halfway up. From here I can see its face better, and I'm sorry for that.

'After all these years,' it says, 'have you finally come to join me in a swim?'

I thought I had, but now that I see it again, I'm afraid. I don't want to ever be anywhere near that creature. I can't say anything.

'No?' it sighs. 'Ah, well. I don't want to swim with you, either. I told you once that there were worse things than being monstrous. I could, for instance, be you.'

I'm about to ask it what it means, but then I think I understand.

'I never sought to be liked, I never sought forgiveness.' I am what I am.

The undermonster blinks. 'You've never belonged here.'

It drops back into the water without a splash, and is gone.

I stand still for perhaps an hour. Waiting.

Eventually, the white shape reappears.

'What do you want of me?' it growls.

I don't know. To take away the need for decisions. I'm tired and bored with life. I want peace.

'Do you want me to kill you, is that it?' It flips over. 'Well, we've had that discussion and I'm not going to. That's a problem you'll have to sort out for yourself.'

And it's gone again.

How long do I wait, standing on that spot among ancient bodies and ancient cobwebs? The wind moves gently and the hulk creaks, weary as me. Bats flit, my breathing slows. I want the undermonster to solve the problem for me. Tiny spiders weave webs between my fingers, then from my shoulders down my arms. The space between my legs is a mass of web. My beard and hair grow, a pair of sparrows makes a nest there. I watch them court, then the female lays her eggs. They hatch, and the pair work furiously to feed their young before my beard trails out off the edge. From time to time, in the blackness, I hear the undermonster splish and splash. Dead bodies are thrown to it and it feeds. And still I do not move. The birds leave, all grown up.

Eventually, the undermonster loses patience. As I knew it would. Nothing can outlast a spiteful old man.

'All right!' It yells. 'Enough of this game!' Then it slides up the rope, slick as a lizard, until its mouth is next to my face, right up against the sole eye it left me with. I move my eyeball, but most of the rest of me is too stiff with disuse to move easily. I'm frightened, I just have no way of showing it.

'You'd like me to eat you,' it snaps. 'You're terrified, oh yes. But still, it's what you want, isn't it? A quick death, without the need for remorse or remembering or decisions.'

The creature stands still. If my heart could remember how, it would be thumping fit to burst my chest. Then the undermonster backs off, perhaps a millimetre, and my fear subsides by the same infinitesimal amount.

'I am still not going to eat you.'

It backs away a little more. Then more.

'But there is a way out for you,' it says.

It backs away completely, revealing a chain leading across the deck, through a hole in the hull, and off down to the water.

'We've been here too long. There's the anchor.'

It flips over the side, its head bobbing back up in front of me.

'It's quite unpleasant down there, but if you go down into the hold, among the bodies you'll find a warspike. That'll do the job.'

After the undermonster drops into the water, I begin to move. It's not easy, after having stood still for so long, but eventually I'm able to get my little finger to wiggle up, and then down, and then up again. The other fingers on that hand follow, then the wrist, then the forearm and elbow, then the rest of the arm to the shoulder.

With one arm free, it's easier to get the second moving. Soon I can turn my waist, and then I pat my legs back into feeling. They creak and complain, especially the knees, but finally they can take a step, bearing my weight, and then another. I don't bother unfreezing my face — what do I need with facial expressions?

Down into the hold I go. The undermonster was right, it is unpleasant. The hold is crammed to the rafters with desiccated bodies, covered in cobwebs and dust. What madness, what murder, took place here? Is this the heart of the University? There are no answers: the undermonster is in the business of doing, not explaining.

At the end of the hold, leaning against a pile of timber that might have been a sea chest, is the warspike. A combination of oversized mallet and armor-piercing spike, these were used in the days when men wore plates of steel into battle. It's probably heavy enough to smash a chain.

I can barely lift the thing: easier by far to drag it back up the stairs. Step by step.

Down the deck to the bows, and there is the chain, held taut for all these years. It looks far too thick for me to break.

I almost laugh at the absurd thought of me, barely able to lift the warspike, smashing the chain.

And yet, I'm able to raise it above my head. There will be little strength, but much gravity, in the swing.

I bring it down, as hard as I can, onto the chain.

I can only blink in surprise as the spike bites through the chain, severing the links. The end attached to the anchor slides away with a splash into the water.

Amazed, I bend down to look at the chain. I didn't think I was that strong. And it turns out that I'm not: the chain was all but rusted through. It was holding together more out of habit than any strength in the metal. I just didn't see that because it was encrusted with dust.

A stiff breeze puffs up. Then I feel a shaking or thrumming through the deck that rises and then drops away.

Around me, the gentle creaking of the ship's timbers has grown louder. It becomes a moaning, and the moaning becomes a noise far worse. Suddenly, I don't want to be on the hulk any more.

Back up the staircase? The feeling in my legs tells me that there is no way I could walk even a few flights any more and, besides, the stones of the stairs have begun to creak too. Looking up, I see the ladder swinging.

I back up to the railing.

A white head, fanged and sardonic, pops up next to me.

'There's a dinghy down here,' it smirks.

Somehow, I scrabble creakily down the ship's rope ladder. From points all across the cavern I can hear splashes. Something large hits the water next to the dinghy as I get in, and I realise that chunks of rock are falling from the ceiling.

The cavern is groaning.

I reach for the oars, but the undermonster has grabbed the bow of the dinghy and is towing it. I sit perfectly still as the creature tows me, faster than I could have rowed, out through the cavern, out and along dark passages, until at last I see the overcast outside light of the University at the end of one of the tunnels.

The dinghy slows and then stops. Ahead, a white hand waves from the surface of the water, and then it slides into the blackness. I catch the flicker of something white and hungry as it streams along, back to the cavern.

Even here, the rock is groaning and straining to move. I can just make out a crack appearing in the ceiling above me. I grab up the oars and slowly, with an old man's painful strokes, make my way down the tunnel and out into the light.

The undermonster has brought me to the side closest to Drab. I row for the shore, for the village, watching the University's great grey flanks all the way.

The stone along the walls lets out great moans, even as the towers shudder, whipping about unlike anything made of stone should. Figures run along the top of the walls in panic. Every so often, the University's seismic twitches bucks one of them off the wall and they fall with a shriek, either grazing the wall before being bounced, dead, into the sea or else falling in alive. There are sharks massing.

I keep rowing, rowing as hard as I can. It's feeble, but what can you do?

There are people running or riding terrified beasts across the great bridge, an exodus. But there are far too many people inside to ever escape at such short notice.

My dinghy beaches itself. I step back, out onto the sandy spit below Drab. Around me, and on the small rise behind, townspeople are congregating: men and women, children and dogs, pointing or barking.

Unable to believe what I see, I take a step and then another into the water. Strong hands grab me and lead me back to the land, speaking soft words of reassurance.

Unimagined! Enormous sails are unfurling, from the myriad towers, slowly sliding into place as huge stone booms settle, hooks bigger than horses sliding into oddly-shaped windows that now reveal their true function. There are groans of wood and stone and metal, monstrous machineries turn, huge swathes of canvas flapping and slowly billowing as the wind begins to rise. A great storm is coming.

Is this what I have done?

People dodge the flapping sails and the enormous ropes that swing and trail through the corridors of the University. Birds, great and black, fill the sky, rising in panic from their perches throughout the University.

Now the sails are set, and with infinite slowness they fill with the wind that grows around us. The sails strain with the wind and that straining is transmitted through the tower-masts to the campus-hull. All pulls to be away, to follow the wind. The forces must be enormous.

There is a sound like a sob. I turn to see the great bridge twisting, people falling off it into the threshing water. And then the bridge comes away from the University, snapping like a twig and crashing down. Those who had not cleared it don't stand a chance.

Having cast off its last mooring, the University begins to sail across the bay. Slowly at first, the hulk inches forward, ropes straining, ancient towers groaning, enormous swathes of ancient canvas holding the wind. Picking up speed as the wind lifts and under full sail, the stone ship goes out into the bay. The villagers of Drab cheer and wish the voyagers well, waving their hats and handkerchiefs. Now making excellent speed, the University crosses the bay, out to the headlands and then past them, beyond our ken, out into the wide world.

And with it departs the overcast sky. For the first time in decades, I feel the sun on my face and on the backs of my hands.

The crowd is silent, beginning to disperse. On the rise, I see two familiar shapes. They have children and grandchildren and even a great-grandchild. Polk sees me and tugs at Mary's arm. They both wave and a strapping fellow, one of their descendants, is despatched to help me up the rise.

As I wait for them to greet me, I think with pleasure that tonight there will be a warm hearth and smiling faces, good cider and good fish stew. There'll be tales to tell and the company of old friends to enjoy. And in the morning, I think with some surprise, there'll be a walk alone to settle the old debts whose details I've forgotten: a tree, and a length of rope.

PANDANUS BOOKS

Pandanus Books was established in 2001 within the Research School of Pacific and Asian Studies (RSPAS) at The Australian National University. Concentrating on Asia and the Pacific, Pandanus Books embraces a variety of genres and has particular strength in the areas of biography, memoir, fiction and poetry. As a result of Pandanus' position within the Research School of Pacific and Asian Studies, the list includes high-quality scholarly texts, several of which are aimed at a general readership. Since its inception, Pandanus Books has developed into an editorially independent publishing enterprise with an imaginative list of titles and high-quality production values.

THE SULLIVAN'S CREEK SERIES

The Sullivan's Creek Series is a developing initiative of Pandanus Books. Extending the boundaries of the Pandanus Books' list, the Sullivan's Creek Series seeks to explore Australia through the work of new writers, with a particular encouragement to authors from Canberra and the region. Publishing history, biography, memoir, scholarly texts, fiction and poetry, the imprint complements the Asia and Pacific focus of Pandanus Books and aims to make a lively contribution to scholarship and cultural knowledge.